CECILIA

CECILIA

K-Ming Chang

COFFEE HOUSE PRESS
Minneapolis
2024

Coffee House Press books are available to the trade through our primary distributor, Consortium Book Sales & Distribution, cbsd.com or (800) 283-3572. For personal orders, catalogs, or other information, write to info@coffeehousepress.org.

Coffee House Press is a nonprofit literary publishing house. Support from private foundations, corporate giving programs, government programs, and generous individuals helps make the publication of our books possible. We gratefully acknowledge their support in detail in the back of this book.

LIBRARY OF CONGRESS CATALOGING-IN-PUBLICATION DATA

Names: Chang, K-Ming, author.
Title: Cecilia / K-Ming Chang.
Description: Minneapolis : Coffee House Press, 2024.
Identifiers: LCCN 2023039642 (print) | LCCN 2023039643 (ebook) | ISBN 9781566897075 (paperback) | ISBN 9781566897082 (epub)
Subjects: LCSH: Women—Fiction. | LCGFT: Queer fiction. | Novellas.
Classification: LCC PS3603.H35733 C43 2024 (print) | LCC PS3603.H35733 (ebook) | DDC 813/.6—dc23/eng /20230919
LC record available at https://lccn.loc.gov/2023039642
LC ebook record available at https://lccn.loc.gov/2023039643

PRINTED IN THE UNITED STATES OF AMERICA

31 30 29 28 27 26 25 24   1 2 3 4 5 6 7 8

The NVLA series is an artistic playground where authors challenge and broaden the outer edges of storytelling. Each novella illuminates the capacious and often overlooked space of possibilities between short stories and novels. Unified by Sarah Evenson's bold and expressive series design, NVLA places works as compact as they are complex in conversation to demonstrate the infinite potential of the form.

"I was almost fifteen now, and the book had filled up. Without my knowing. With a senile girlhood."

>—*Fleur Jaeggy*, Sweet Days of Discipline
>*(translated by Tim Parks)*

"Who hasn't ever wondered: am I a monster or is this what it means to be a person?"

>—*Clarice Lispector*, The Hour of the Star
>*(translated by Benjamin Moser)*

"Let me make my offering on the altar of—absence. The eyes that would have understood are closed."

>—*Dorothy Strachey*, Olivia

CECILIA

I saw Cecilia again when I turned twenty-four and switched jobs for the third time that year. In the laundry room of the chiropractor's office, I folded four types of towels and three sizes of gowns, my fingers sidling along seams and clawing the lint screen clean. The towels, which were stored in white laminate cabinets and laid out on the examination tables, had to be folded into fourths and rolled thick as thighs. The fraying ones were retired to a metal shelf along the back wall, a columbarium for cloth. I mourned them all: the aging towels were the easiest to fold, to flatten. They were softer and thinner and hung like pigskin over my forearm, clinging directly to my meat, nursing on my heat. They didn't get lumpy or beady when I tucked them, and their pleats never pickled into permanence, never stiffened into ridges.

The laundry room was a windowless space at the back of the clinic, painted pink and white like pork belly. I only ever saw the chiropractor and the receptionist when they entered to use the employee toilet in the closet next to the dryer. The chiropractor's peeing was astonishingly loud, almost symphonic, resonating inside the walls and harmonizing with the retching of the washer. His stream was so insistent, so unflagging, that I sometimes imagined it siphoned directly into the pipes at the back of the washer. It was his piss that filled the machine, battering the glass window, seasoning the sheets. That would solve the mystery of the sheets on the gyrating table, which yellowed too quickly even when I bleached them in the sink, turning the insides of my wrists translucent. The gyrating table was my name for the uncanny contraption in treatment room two, the largest of the rooms. Once or twice the chiropractor had attempted to demonstrate its function to me, even inviting me to try it out myself. It was like a dentist's chair, slanted at a forty-five-degree angle, its cushions made of foam and green pleather, except you were supposed to lie on it face down, and once you were cupped to its cutting-board surface, it began to rotate and twist and tip and rock and hum and sometimes even shudder. The chiropractor turned it on with a remote control and explained to me that its movements were expertly calibrated, allowing him to deliver the correct amounts of pressure to targeted areas without straining himself or distorting his own spine—but when it was empty, whirring without any body, it looked to me like a severed tongue, a fish flailing to speak. It wriggled in the dark like antennae, trying to tune in to a language it had lost. When I sprayed it down after appointments, patting its glossy flank to soothe it, convincing it not to buck anyone, I squinted at its stillness and imagined what word it wanted to say.

Unlike the chiropractor, the receptionist peed so discreetly that I found myself inching toward the door after she locked it, perching my ear against the thin plywood, listening for the rattle of her bladder. But I never heard anything, not even the shriek of her zipper or the applause of the toilet seat lowering, not even the sound of the faucet fidgeting. I imagined that her pee was like the rain in movies, a shimmering sheet so embedded in the scene that you could no longer distinguish its rhythm from the voices in the foreground, the faces feathering the screen. A rain like bestial breathing. A few times I became so entranced I forgot to flee, and when she opened the door, I was standing there with my ears flexed like wings. I pretended I'd been waiting for the bathroom myself, but I could tell she didn't believe it, and she avoided speaking to me except to let me know when a patient had left. She began turning on the faucet while she pissed, and the sounds were unsortable, threading together into the weather. When it was time to address me, she knocked on the laundry room door, competing with the sound of towels fistfighting in the dryer, and said, *Get the room*. This was my cue to wipe down the tables and replace the towels and gather the soiled laundry.

In addition to doing the laundry, which overfilled the hampers and slumped like dead birds on every surface, I mopped the floors, vacuumed the rooms, and cleaned the patient and employee bathrooms. I refilled the soap dispenser in the patient bathroom, which dribbled like a nosebleed, its residue jellying on the rim of the sink. Every hour, I sponged away the gum. The toilet bowl turned brown because of mineral buildup, and although I scrubbed it daily, it always looked like someone had recently stewed their shit in it. The toilet-paper dispenser was broken and had to be bandaged with Scotch tape.

When I stirred the brush inside the bowl, I heard the contents of my own bladder sloshing, slapping all the walls of my body. I became aware that I needed to use the bathroom, but I abstained. I liked to see how long I could wait. My bladder stiffened into bone and became my fist. It tautened into a grape of pain.

The chiropractor claimed that at his busiest, he saw over one hundred patients a day, and though I never knew if this was true, never saw anyone coming or going, I gathered the aftermath of their bodies: alcohol-soggy cotton balls sunken in the trash cans, paper towels souping in the sink, handprints of sweat gilding the tables, bouquets of dark hair arranged in the chamber of my vacuum cleaner. Though the job was full time, the chiropractor said he'd only take me on as an independent contractor, which I knew was just a way of saying I'd have no benefits. My brother told me those were the best kinds of jobs: make sure they pay in cash, he said, you won't have to pay taxes. He collected bills from handyman gigs and rolled them into sausages, encasing them in socks that were sweat-encrusted and mildewed—a natural repellent against thieves. In my family, we weaponized our stench.

It was Wednesday when I saw Cecilia. Unlike the receptionist, who had to keep track of appointment dates, I never knew the day of the week or whether it was winter, though it was winter. In the windowless room, it was always warm, and the wet fluorescent light flicked my earlobes with its tongue. At work, all conscious thought was caught in the mesh screen of my mind and balled away, and what remained was the beeping of the machine when it was done or overloaded, my fingers groping for corners, the volcanic power of the chiropractor's piss as it plundered the pipes and grew gold roots beneath my feet. My only aspiration was to expel myself that fluently. On his best days, there was no trickling or tapering off: it ended as abruptly as it began, the stream severed cleanly as if it were snipped.

I learned it was Wednesday because the chiropractor, after exiting the bathroom that morning, turned to me and said, *A lot of new patients today, and on a Wednesday.* He said nothing else, and the words caught in my mind's screen, separate from my living. Inside this room I was ghostly, a fly's wing, leashed to the light above me. I folded to the rhythm of *on a Wednesday*, pluralizing each pleat, manufacturing halves and then quarters, rolling and stacking, bending and filling.

The receptionist knocked twice, *Get the room,* so I abandoned the hand towel I was using to wipe the window of the washer, leaving it to puddle on top of the machine.

The treatment rooms lined a narrow carpeted hallway, rows of sliding doors on either side. Unless you dislocated the doors a little, jiggling them in their sockets, they didn't slide shut properly, or they made a metallic scraping sound that turned your spine to slime. When the doors were left half open, it was a sign for me to enter and clean the room as quickly as possible, without jostling the requisite plastic spine model. Each vertebra was labeled with a number, the spaces between them glowing like keyholes, inviting any finger to try and unlock them. As much as possible, I liked to face the spine while I cleaned; if I didn't keep an eye on it, I heard the bones jingling like forks. They pricked my skin, took bites of my mind.

The door to treatment room two was open. It was the largest room and had its own gravity, holding the gyrating table in its orbit, and I braced myself for that giant tongue, that half-born word. The room was dimmed to let me know it was dirty, and I entered so quickly that for several steps, for a handful of feathered seconds, I didn't notice there was someone still inside. I walked toward the cabinet where the bottles of cleaner were kept, the neon liquid sloshing like the acid in my belly. Only when I began to kneel did I see the bright piping of a gown, a hem I had flipped in the right direction, a slight heat still wafting from it.

My head jerked up, and I saw her standing directly in front of the spine model, the table tilted behind her, slick and poised to speak. Her diamonded gown was glowing, so dew-clean that the hallway light clung to her front, and I climbed the lattice of its pattern before reaching her face.

It was a face I had dusted off in my memory so frequently that seeing it now, in the present, made me wonder if this one was a bootleg, if the original had been destroyed to keep me from corrupting it. Her long hair was loose, which was unusual for patients, who were asked to arrive with their hair tied back so the chiropractor could traverse the full territory of their spines. She wore her gown unknotted, the strings limp at her sides like desiccated insect limbs. Her posture seemed perfect to me, not at all like the stance of someone who needed to see a chiropractor, who experienced gravity. A shadow clogged the doorway, and I glanced behind me to see if it was the receptionist or the chiropractor, telling me to hurry up or leave.

When I turned back around, she had taken a step closer to me. Her legs and feet were bare, the gown bunching at her sides, and I tried not to imagine what she looked like from behind. Though she was technically facing me, I felt her true gaze was pointing behind her. The opening in her gown was a flickering eyelid. I looked at the wall behind her, avoiding her face, knowing that it had changed since I last saw her. I didn't want to look at it now, to reinstate the years between us. I wanted to turn and flee. I wanted the intimacy of distance, to be far enough away to see her entire surface.

Her heat hemmed me in, electrified the air. She was smiling, and her teeth were a single rind of light. I stood slowly, shifting away from their sour radius. The fresh towels clamped in my armpits were slopping out of shape, expanding in the steam of my sweat.

You remember me, she said. She didn't say her name. Because I didn't know how to answer, I stepped back toward the door and said I was sorry, I'd leave her to undress. *When you leave,* I told her, *you can leave the door cracked. The lobby is straight ahead.*

Cecilia didn't move. Though the room was sapped of light, her shadow lapped at the floor, licking up my ankles. From where did her shadow summon its water?

She tilted her head, an unfamiliar motion. Cecilia's movements were never minor, and this slight angling was so foreign that for a second I was comforted, wondering if I'd mistaken someone else for her.

But then she approached me. The spine model shifted into view as she stepped forward, which gave me the strange impression that she'd left her bones behind. That her spine was standing in its previous place, fully assembled, and only the sheet of her skin dangled in front of me.

It was her face. Her narrow chin, which I'd envied. Glistening as if I'd licked it. Even in this dim, I could see the canopy of her lashes, trapping any light that tried to reach her eyes. Because they could not reflect anything, her eyes were quiet as an animal's, turned inward, preoccupied with the darkness inside her own skull. She still had the mole underneath her left eye, protruding slightly like a nipple, which she'd tried to scrape off with her mother's As Seen on TV vegetable peeler and which had grown back identical, though she'd claimed it came back larger, fat enough to nurse on. I could see the color of her nipples through the gown. I ducked my head. Patients weren't required to remove their underwear. The more I looked at her nipples, the more they widened like rings of displaced water, seeping across the front of her gown until I wondered if she was bleeding.

She itched her wrist, dredging up flecks of dried skin. She used to say she would someday scatter her own ashes. The impossibility of this act only strengthened the promise. Many times in my life, I had seen someone across the street or out the bus window, scraping plaque off the roots of their kumquat tree or laughing open mouthed at a flippant cloud or frothing from both nostrils while arguing with a stranger, and the way they were moving their hands and arms—with a fledgling's awkwardness, elbows crooking like wings—disturbed me into indigestion. Only much later would I realize: my sickness was the shock of seeing her shadow appropriated, her behavior plagiarized.

You look the same, she said. Her voice was lower. She glanced down, and it was the first time I realized she was uncertain about how to address me. She rolled her lower lip between her teeth, and I watched it ripple and shine with spit, the slug of my love.

I'll change, she said, *I just really like this room.*

I was surprised. The room was so familiar to me I no longer saw anything in it—it was too staged, shaped like a room but not a room, the poster of a seaside view on one wall, the green glass lamp in the corner, the filters combing out the air. Only the motored table remained alive in my mind. I tried to imagine her magnetized to it, her body flung in elliptical orbits, her knees bouncing on the cushions. But when I thought of her lying on the table face down, I could only see her steering it, paddling it out into the day.

Cecilia turned around, ushering the scent of her sweat into the air, the loose curtains of her gown fluttering open in the back. Her skin was so sudden. The white elastic of her underwear, bare as bone, snapped against my throat. I recoiled and scurried out the door, the walls of the narrow hallway grating my shoulders, whittling me down. Behind me, I heard the door scraping shut.

My heart wrung itself out, and I felt the blood return to my wrists and hands and head. Two more knocks on the laundry room door, two more rooms cleared out, and treatment room two was still shut. No light sludging out the crack of its door, but I didn't want to knock, so I waited until the receptionist let me know that room two needed getting. When I returned to it, I saw that the door was indeed cracked, but so slightly that only a thumb would fit in the gap. That was how she defined an opening.

I cleaned the room slower than usual, searching for a raft of stray hairs or some message she'd left for me. I even checked the ceiling. It would have never occurred to me to do this, except Cecilia used to enter a room with her chin tilted upward, pining for light. But when I looked up, I only saw shadows. Spores speckled the ceiling, fuzzing the light fixture. Repulsed, I lowered my head and knew I would never be able to enter this room again without thinking of the pelt above, thickening by the minute, begging to be petted. Even as I shuddered, I imagined stroking the spores: a row of nipples stiffening.

No message was left behind for me. Only the pile of used towels on the table, the gown flickering on top of it, stirred slightly by the air-conditioning. The gown's fabric was starchy, the way the chiropractor preferred it, soft only at the armpits and around the neckline, where her sweat and heat might have congregated. I balled it up and tucked it under my left arm, then bundled the towels to bring to the laundry room. When I got back, I sorted only the towels into their correct hampers. The gown I tossed onto the folding table behind me, where the clean laundry was stacked into obelisks. Though I turned my back to the gown, I felt its presence cleaving to me, felt its sleeve holes whimpering for my wrists.

After stacking a load of dry towels, still hot enough to scald my fingertips, I turned back to the gown and lifted it, my nose roaming the fabric. It was bright as the leaf-brittle dryer sheets we used, even at the armpits. I tried to decide if the side seams were damp or just cold. I fluttered the gown flat on the table, looked around quickly, and bent to lick its loins. Like a bird chewing dew, my tongue dabbed at the diamonds patterning the crotch. The cloth was so devoid of flavor that it didn't even taste clean: it was simply the fabric of absence. It hadn't lived long enough on her skin to remember anything.

The chiropractor walked into the laundry room, and I shook out the gown and fiddled with the strings, pretending to be pleating it. When I stepped away, my lips lurked in its folds. But the chiropractor didn't look at me, just headed straight to the bathroom. He flicked the switch, and the light lagged a few seconds before limping in. I saw his shadow coloring in the crack under the door. His piss trumpeted into the toilet, louder than I'd ever heard it. Then it thinned into a hiss, managing a few percussive beats before tapering into silence.

Cecilia was the one who first told me: *Boys hold their dicks when they pee, isn't that gross?* We were thirteen and sitting on the curb together, waiting for the city bus. Whenever it arrived, jerking toward us, we made a game of seeing how long we could stay seated before its wheels severed our knees. Cecilia could wait the longest, the bus lunging toward her, the soles of her feet stapled to the street. I would watch the street while she watched the sky, refusing to move until the bus poured its shadow over her head. Then she would retract her legs and roll backward, bouncing up from the pavement.

When she told me this fact, I was so horrified that I didn't believe her. *Haven't you noticed,* she said, *that you can never see a man's hands when he pees? That they're always in front, like they're watering something? Guess what they're holding.* With a jolt, I realized this was true. My brother peed with the door open, the only one in our family of women, and from behind, I'd never once seen his hands. He was never holding a book in front of him, or holding a phone to his ear, or simply allowing his hands to slack off at his sides.

It seemed so impossible that I stopped watching the street. If this were true, it had to happen often, boys touching their penises. I'd never once touched myself while peeing, or even while not peeing. The idea hadn't even occurred to me, touching. Underwear touched you. Toilet paper touched you, brief as a bee. But the directness of a hand was different. I thought everyone went their entire lives never directly touching the places they peed from, and when Cecilia repeated what she'd said, I still couldn't believe it. *They touch it every time?* I said. Cecilia looked at the sky and laughed and said they had to. To direct it. The fact that it was a necessary and casual utility—like holding back your hair to drink from a water fountain— shocked me more than anything. It seemed grotesque and barbaric, designed purely to disgust me. But beneath my disgust was a constant awe, the kind Cecilia must have felt when she found a dead squirrel on our street, its flesh freed from the bone by a family of crows.

That is the worst thing I have ever heard, I said to Cecilia. *That means they touch it every few hours!* She smiled at me and reined in her legs, and I realized too late that the bus was lurching toward us. But we were linked at the elbows, and she pulled me up with her. We boarded the bus together, and I looked at the hands of every man inside it. Seven. Some were tall or old or ghosts. I looked at their hands for some visible evidence of savagery, moles or scales or knuckles poking out like horns. I waited for their hands to be let off their arms, free to sneak inside any skin.

Inside this bus, Cecilia and I were careful to touch very little. Our mothers warned us about the infectiousness of death. Even a safety railing or a bus strap could sicken us, so we pretended to be taxidermy, stiff and leaning against each other. I kept counting hands as they entered and exited, as they touched windows and green plastic seats and nostrils filled with moss and jean pockets and earlobes. There wasn't skin between anything. The sky slipped and exposed the moon, and I wished Cecilia hadn't told me the thing she knew. I wanted to know what was safe to look at.

When I got home, I sat down on the toilet. I listened to my piss prattle in the pipes, repeating her name. I didn't touch anything but the toilet paper knotting in my sweaty fist, the bar of soap made of dog's drool, the faucet spraying spittle, the frayed towel Ama mended once in a while. I was reassured by ritual. I inscribed my borders clearly. It didn't matter if Cecilia was telling the truth, I decided, as long as I could inventory my touch, as long as I didn't slip from my silhouette.

I kept my hands light, stuffing them with feathers and puppeting them in public, teaching them to flit from surface to surface. But they were not alone: they were hunted by another pair of hands, ghost hands grown in the darkness of my body, slicking out of me and into the toilet bowl. Shiny and skinless as organs. When they reached for me, I shut the lid and flushed.

That night, I lay in bed between Ma and Ama. Their creek of sweat hollowed out the valley where I slept. My hands doubled on each wrist, and I felt the weight of both pairs burdening the air, pulping my pelt, smearing me into the sheets. The knowledge of touch was touch.

• • •

The day I saw Cecilia again, I took my usual lunch break in the alley behind the clinic, where the strip mall's dumpster squatted in a chain-link cage. Later I'd come back with the trash from the treatment rooms. Crows clung to the dumpster cage, beaks plunging through the mesh, fencing for anything edible. Their eyes and plumage were so dark and matte they looked like absences, holes snipped into fabric. They moved together as the sky's liquid layer. What I admired most about them was that no matter how scattered they were, hundreds of their bodies beading the branches or sprinkling the roofs, their calls synced together until they sounded like a single body. I imagined their throats bound into a bouquet. Their beaks drilling into the base of my throat, twisting out the bars of my bones. When I opened my mouth to speak, there was only the caw of crows.

As I leaned against the concrete wall and tilted my head, a new flock careened into the cage, beaks burrowing into its holes. They were trying to unknot the fence, and a few aluminum wires were already snipped, dangling like the strings of a gown. The staggered calls of the new flock congregated into a single cry, the one that tumbles from your lungs when you're born.

A few of the crows on the top of the cage seemed to be watching me, tilting their heads, though I couldn't confirm this, since their eyes were indistinguishable from their plumage. But if they were, it was because the chiropractor had told me to shoot them with a green laser pointer he'd bought online and kept in the laundry room. The crows would wait on rooftops, then descend into the alley and the parking lot, their presence an infestation, and he'd read online that crows were repulsed by green light. I hadn't believed him at first, but when he instructed me to scare them away from his dumpster, I took the laser pointer outside and arrowed the sky with its light. Because I was afraid of blinding them, I aimed at the crows' chests. They reeled as if shot, screaming as they scrambled up the sky. When they landed on a neighboring roof, I swore they stayed close to record my face, printing my image on the undersides of their wings, confirming me in their chest cavities. I'd read somewhere that crows could recognize faces for years, another fact I hadn't believed. They were watching me now, beginning to squawk out of sync, reminded of the light I weaponized. Then the whole flock lifted off, dyeing every strand of the sky.

Cecilia's hair was the color of those wings, so dark it sipped the light out of rooms, rubbed off on the night. I imagined her walking across the parking lot out front, loose hair caught in a cloud's fist, her body bouncing up and down as the cloud jerked her around. The alley was too narrow for clouds. I imagined her spine left behind on the table of treatment room two, laid out like a pearl necklace. I wondered what she remembered.

· · ·

When I went home it was just past nine, and Ma and Ama were watching TV in the living room of our apartment, the one we'd been renting since before I was born. The duplexes on our street were split into front and back, and their interiors were mapped differently: In the front units, the bathrooms and kitchens were planted far apart. In the back units, each toilet sat in a closet at the end of the kitchen counter. *The toilet is so close to the stove,* Ama joked, *you can cook the food and then slide your meal straight in. Bypass the body entirely! Forget digestion, it's too slow! Save time and expedite the process. Everything you eat is going to end up in the toilet anyway.*

Through our thin bedroom wall, we could eavesdrop on the front unit. We heard the Nings boiling broths, taking showers, and chasing each other around the kitchen. The Nings fought so often Ma said their shouting was more regular than their shitting. It was true that we never heard their toilets flush, and yet we heard them yelling every morning. Unlike the Nings, we were rarely constipated, and no one got hit by Ma. She said this was because Ama used to hit her. One time, after it rained, Ma wanted to roll in the mud, and Ama broke Ma's ankle to keep her from getting her dress dirty. It was a special dress printed with butterflies. After that, Ma made a promise that if she ever gave birth to something, she would love it as lightly as a fly landing on a cow's ass. A love you feel instinctually, the way a cow always knows when there's a fly on its ass. But the fly will never bruise the cow's ass or permanently attach itself. *Because the culmination of every relationship is separation. It's death. Every relationship is just practice for parting.* I admired Ma's devotion to detachment, her belief in severance as the only certainty, though I refused this faith. To me, love was lodging yourself in the wall between two units, growing in the dark like a mushroom. The three of us could cling there forever and feed on moisture, undiscovered. Death was no reason to separate.

The living room was dark except for the TV screen. Our landlord still didn't know about the peach-faced lovebird Ama kept in a cage on top of the TV, and I warned Ama that the lovebird would probably go deaf if it continued living there. *If nothing's lopped off our ears yet,* Ama said, gesturing at the ceiling and the sky above, where airplanes swung like hatchets at our heads, *then nothing ever will.*

The lovebird's face was red as an opera mask. Red down its neck and chest too, like a slit throat. It clung to the side of its cage and rattled the bars with its beak, but Ama told me to ignore it, it was just upset the door was locked with a paper clip, but she'd had to do it, because last night it escaped and started flying around our bedroom, and your mother nearly zapped it out of the air with the electric flyswatter, luckily she recognized that it was too fat to be a fly or a mosquito, can you imagine a mosquito that size, how much blood would be inside it, I knew a few mosquitos that size, barges of blood, so full they don't even fly away, they can't even move, but there aren't mosquitos here, thank god, and the ones that are here are so skinny-hungry.

When I approached the cage to refill the lovebird's dish of red-dyed melon seeds, it cracked open its beak and stabbed at me, bridled only by the bars. Though I shied away, Ama always said it wouldn't hurt me. They were naturally territorial, she said, but they were a prey species.

There are two species in the world, Ama used to explain. Predators and prey. Everyone is born from one of these two lineages, and you can't predict which. Whether your parents are prey or predators doesn't matter. It's a combination of factors, and history isn't the only handle on it. When I asked Ama how you knew which one you were, and what it meant to be predator or prey, she didn't explain. She only said it was as inevitable as a baby growing molars. Whatever you are will emerge and announce itself, like sugar in your pee. Like blood lifted up by a cut.

I wedged myself between Ma and Ama, careful not to kick over the mug of sunflower seeds sitting between the sofa feet. Our sofa was swathed in towels to protect its surface from stains and the erosive properties of sunlight and air and voices. But because the towels absorbed our sweat, Ama complained that it felt like sitting in a giant diaper. Still, we never uncovered the sofa, and I asked Ma if it wasn't defeating the point, covering something to keep it clean: if it was always sheathed, how would anyone know if it was clean or not? And what was the point of having a nice sofa if it was going to stay unseen? But Ma shook her head and said it wasn't about seeing. *It's about knowing what you keep clean,* Ma said. *You don't have to see what's underneath. You don't have to touch something to love it.*

I settled in one of the craters, and Ma turned to touch the ends of my shoulder-length hair, saying she would cut it again for me soon, she knew I liked it chin-length, that I didn't want long hairs clinging like worms to white towels, I wanted something easy to pluck from a surface, how about even shorter this time, like hers? I looked at Ma and said no, I didn't mind it this length for a while. Cecilia's hair today was about the length of mine, but on her it looked longer, long enough to play our old game of horses, our hair yanked like reins, our jaws clamping pencils like bits.

Ma and Ama were wearing their matching baby-blue uniforms, both ready for the night shift at the retirement home. *Leave some sleep for us,* they always said before leaving. Though Ama was old enough to be a resident there, she dyed her short hair black and set it with curlers, wrapped her knees in drugstore bandages, left her cane on the sofa—she didn't allow us to call it a cane, and instead said it was an anti-mugger defense weapon—and told me retirement was a recent invention.

You're born, you work, you die, you receive your next life, she said. *Living has to come in between.*

I sat between them on the vinyl sofa, my head shelved on Ma's shoulder, her fingers rolling my left earlobe, the place where my headaches were planted. She stunted the pain, pinched it tiny as a sesame seed, swallowed it for me. On TV, the local news was reporting on the annual winter crow infestation, how one downtown street in a neighboring city was so flooded with crows that they descended on shoppers and diners, causing local businesses to issue complaints. The city promised intervention, advocating for humane removal of the crows, and on screen, a man in a khaki vest explained that crow population growth was directly proportional to human population growth. *They follow the same slope,* he said, and his finger traced a diagonal line. *Parallel populations.* When I remembered the dumpster in its cage, the garbage bins disassembled by their beaks, I thought that if they ate our waste, we must eat something of theirs too. We must feed on their white feces. We must live off their loathing. They must provide our lives, stitching us a night. *Crows have a sense of vengeance,* Ma said: A woman she worked with at the home had once knocked down a crow's nest. All its babies were boiled tender as onions in the sun. After that, the crows scalped the woman in her sleep, her skull emerging like a moon. *Now she wears wigs,* Ma explained to me, *and she also had to move.*

TV light filled the dimple in Ma's left cheek, the same one Ama had: On Ma, it appeared when she was hungry or missed someone. On Ama, it appeared when she laughed or was constipated.

Bookended by their bodies, I fell asleep and woke up to the empty sofa. A note had been written directly onto my palm: My brother was at a furnace repair job and would come home soon. Dinner was on the stove, braised meat, shoelaces of tofu. The house was dark except for the muted TV, now playing the bright shards of a traffic accident as the lovebird tucked its head under its wing to sleep.

In the dark, I slipped the gown I'd taken home out of my shoulder bag. It looked smaller in this room where I was alone. Cecilia once asked me why there was a living room but no dying room, and I told her that no one wanted a dying room. It would be scary and a waste of space. And what would go in it? We knew the things you needed to live: money for food, a blanket, a mother or two. But what would you need to die?

Now that I was alone with her gown, the fabric cold and calcifying, I realized she had only been asking for symmetry. A living room and a dying room. A morning and a moon. Thirst and a fist. This gown delivered me symmetry: it was equivalent to her absence these past ten years, its skin the same thickness as silence. In the dark, I undressed to my underwear and threaded my arms through the fabric, knotting the strings behind me. It was tighter on me, clinging rather than flapping, hem itching my shins. My sweat gathered in the gutter of my spine, and I tried not to let it dampen the gown. The white fabric was a blank screen. When I stood before the TV, images of crows were projected onto my torso, their wings chopping up my belly.

I walked to the bedroom and knelt on my futon. Crawling beneath my lint-crumbed blanket, I fell asleep inside her skin. My dreams repeated: she stood before me, her skin an open gown, her bones fleeting, a flock of white birds, a flock of salt. Each of her teeth was a crow's beak. She sipped fat from the rinsed dishes of my kneecaps. I knelt in front of an open cabinet, and she stood above in her glowing gown. When I stood up and reached for her, she flung herself back as if shot, a green laser beam needling through her left nipple. Through her gown, I saw her nipples. Someone should warn her, I thought. I stood in front of the caged dumpster where crows collided into each other, so eager to escape me, knowing my face as a shorthand for hurt, remembering. Did she remember? I wanted to ask, but she clutched the green beam and yanked it out of her black-feathered breast. I bit my tongue, cradled the blood. I didn't deserve to look at her. The crows had a name for me, their glossy bodies battered in the washing machine, their eyes loose beads, flung in handfuls against the front-loading window. Guilt powdered my mouth like glass. I bit down on my bladder, soliciting piss. The crows had a name for everything they remembered. She called my name from behind the half-cracked door, from inside my bladder. Hurry, I thought, get the gown off before you wet it. It is already. Her voice in my bladder again, filling it up with pebbles, a pouch of her panting. *Careful,* she said, *get me out of here.* I lay face up and naked on my bed, the gown parted, fingernails poised over my intestines, my bladder. But I didn't know how to peck her an opening without soiling her, without spilling my piss over her head like a wedding veil. With my nails, I danced on the roof of her skull, grating her into rain.

• • •

No memory is mutual, but I pray you've kept this one under my name:

It's summer, hot enough to cremate the days. Hours turn to ash in our mouths. You teach me how to transform my spit into fish, but mine always die gasping in the gutter. Only yours can survive outside the waters of the body. Bend over the gutter and show me: your spit unfurling, sizzling when it hits the tarred street, frying your name in its grease.

In the gutter, your spit is parceled into pearls that elongate into tadpoles, fins writhing up from their jellied spines. The sunlight sequins them into fish, and they swim together, without any need for water or rain, each as long as your pinky. You have pretty pinkies, the kind that look like they should be hinged to a doll, the knuckles only accessories. My pinkies are thick and calloused, born to burrow inside fists, born to be drumsticks, and I beg you to gnaw them off me, spit them into the gutter so they'll live again as fish.

The spit-fish fabricate a river as they follow the length of the gutter, and I wonder where they're headed, if they are migrating to give birth or die, if they will return someday to lay my eggs in your mouth. That was the year both our grandfathers returned to the island to live off their veterans' pensions for a few months before full-time ghosthood. It was you who told me that once a body is cremated, it isn't instantly ash. The fire only flays the flesh, and all your calcium endures, even toothaches, even joint pain. You come out like crispy cookies on a dish. A platter of hips and diamond-hard shits. Stacking you inside the urn, they organize your bones in order, from the floor up: your footbones at the bottom, then your vertebrae in ascending notes, then the lid of your skull crowning the pile. They standardize skeletons, correct the posture of spirits. If you want to be buried under a tree or foster a flower's knees, you have to be put in the grinder, grated into ash as fine as pepper. But that's just if you prefer to season something.

The knowledge of that extra step upset me. I thought we were all naturalized into ash, that heat was all we needed to be free. But you reminded me of the grinder, of a jawbone. You reminded me that disintegration was labor, chewing before swallowing. Our bones resist becoming nothing.

From my agong, I inherited my liver, which was sawed out of his body and now bobbed in a jar next to the kitchen sink. From your agong, you inherited spit that could turn into fish. Your agong was a soldier, but he never killed anyone. Mostly he gambled and read books, though he preferred his women illiterate. *Men need to think you're the lesser species,* Ma always said to me, *but really, men never grow up. Their mothers take care of them, then their wives, and then death delivers them all over again. Girls are born grown up. They're like little balls of knotted yarn, nothing makes them happy. And we have to act for the men, act like we need them, like those birds that pretend to be injured, dragging their wings to lure predators from their nests. We have to spend our whole lives luring them away from our real minds.*

Your agong's throat was always clogged with carp. Fish with scholarly faces. Fragrant fish with jade-translucent eyes and scales that could have been someone's sky. Your mother said he was unevolved, always uprooting the family to follow his whims, never considering the consequences. Because of this, he began to resemble the sea, where all of us lived before we became human, before we had limbs. I wondered if you were an original life-form, a root we all grew from. A creature so careless, it lost the concept of death.

One year he vomited sardines for a month straight, a bucket of saltwater under his bed to keep them alive for the night. The next morning, they could be fried. Another year he spat milkfish onto the street and caused six-car pileups. The milkfish were too slippery to drive on, but we loved to strap them to the soles of our feet and skate all the way to the freeway.

At the entrance of the freeway were crosses made of Popsicle sticks, marking the places where people had been struck and killed. We wanted to die there too, at the entrance of something, we didn't want to be sequestered in rooms, we wanted a public passing, so we made crosses out of Popsicle sticks and jabbed them into each other's stomachs. Our dead were not buried beneath crosses. They were ashes. They were aquatic. Their souls reincarnated into the bodies of flies and fish. Their suffering and happiness outgrew all landmasses, spilling into the sky and the sea. We strapped fish to our feet and sledded on their silver sides until they pulped, pink innards balling beneath our feet, eyes skidding like dropped pennies. We sucked the slender bones out of each other's soles, the quills clear as rain, and sometimes I accidentally pushed them in deeper, shunting them into the flesh of your foot, threading them up toward your throat.

The truth is that I wanted to obliterate you. My dreams were blistered with fish I fried in pans of my sweat, fish whose mouths I thumbed open, inserting both my fists until their jaws crackled and splintered into light. You told me once that all girls are born with a baby in each limb, but only the one in the belly survives, because only that one is fed. For years I was haunted by this, and thought of the dead lodged in my limbs, giving each one a surname. How unfair, I thought, that only the baby in the belly can breathe, the only one with direct pipelines to light, tethered to a hole on both ends. I was willing to begin at either one, your asshole or your mouth, I wanted any way inside of you, but I kept outgrowing your openings. Every time you offered proximity, a hand on my thigh, an elbow hooked through mine, I refused to forfeit into liquid. Yet I envied your spit in the gutter, its instinct to swim upstream to the place where it would perish among its young. Outside of you, I flapped like a fish evicted.

Once, in the year of the sardines, when you were sick of the fish oil sopping your sheets, sheening the ceiling, you told me that mouth holes and nose holes and ear holes and eye holes are all basically the same thing, all leading to the same bedroom. You said that when your agong was asleep in front of the muted TV, you listened to the news through his nasal cavity, talked to your aunts through his ears, and chatted to weathermen in his throat. I didn't believe you, because if all those holes were doors to the same room, then why didn't everything get confused? When you breathed through your nose, why didn't it inflate your bowels? When I swallowed in your presence, why didn't my eyes cry saliva? Why didn't I lose a tooth looking at you?

You had no proof to show me, except that when you cried—if I had yanked too hard on your hair playing horses, if I had thrust the fishbone deeper into your heel instead of showing it out—saltwater unmoored your mind. Your brain bobbed and hit the ceiling of your skull. I pressed my ear to the top of your head whenever you chewed or spoke or cried, and inside, I could hear the place I came from. I read later that all of us have an inner fish, all of us have symptoms from the sea. It was only when we crawled onto land that we, as organisms, developed poor vision. We saw better when we lived in water. I only knew I was alive inside you.

Now only my urine is related to the ocean. Though I originate from you, I cannot return. The urge to enter you has been replaced by the need to empty. I know my lineage: when I piss, the rope of it pulls me down into the toilet, threads me through the exit, and when I flush, I disappear with it. I open my eyes in the night of a pipe and feel only the narrowness of nearing you, the velocity of your swallow. My fist thrusts through a fish, reaching for the gape of your lips. Gown me in guts. Sleeve me with your spit. I will twirl in a skirt of sirloin. I will wear my violence wider than sky.

• • •

When I woke up, the gown had unknotted in my sleep and twisted around me. It was wet everywhere, a heavier wetness than sweat, and when I sat up and realized how empty I felt, how light between the legs, I realized I'd pissed myself.

The curtains were yanked away from the window, light sagging the glass. Ama and Ma had already gone to tend to other bodies, and their bedsheets were mounded into a steaming burrow. I wanted their heat to protect me. I prayed they hadn't smelled my leaking. Rolling off my futon, I bundled my sheets and the gown in my arms, shrouded myself in the white nightgown Ama had slopped on the ground, and walked toward the side yard, where a communal washing machine squatted on the concrete. Ama's nightgowns were lace collared and expansive as ghosts. She clothed herself in their moans. Long ago, Ama used to sew handkerchiefs of the same texture and fabric and sell them at bus stops. *Someone always needs to sneeze when they get off the bus,* Ama said, *it's all that exhaust.* When the body is swinging, its cavities are rattled, and phlegm and spit loosen like ribbons. They dangle out of all your openings.

Years ago, I spotted a dog-sized crow on top of the washing machine. At first, I thought it was injured or going rabid: it hopped on one foot, then the other, then the other, wings half-open, head bobbing up and down, body crouched as it bounced off the low ceiling of a lightless sky. It carried its beak around like a trumpet, slanting it skyward but making no sound. It appeared to be laughing. I watched it for a long time before realizing it was not suffering. It was playing. It leapt off the washing machine and scampered across the side yard, flicking its wings and fanning its tail. It was the most uncanny thing I'd ever seen, more terrifying than the time I saw a stray dog in our neighborhood squeeze a dead possum so tightly in its jaws that its intestines squirted out of its ass. The crow's behavior disturbed me because it had never occurred to me that wild animals could be playful. That they did things that were not purely utilitarian or appetite driven. I thought playing was the privilege of the domesticated: dogs chasing their own tails, housecats hunting beams of light. I was suddenly aware that I had no idea what crows, or any animals, were doing to their days. I'd only ever felt safe because I assumed they were eating, hunting, being hunted, shitting, scenting. Adhering to an order I understood, like the one Ama described: You're born. You leave your family before it can eat you. You are eaten by another family and give birth to its children. You make your life a service to others, and in exchange you are never alone with your desires. Now I realized that these creatures could do anything outside my imagining, do things for illegible reasons, and this knowledge knelt on my chest for an entire morning. I left the week's laundry outside, forgotten like a carcass. The more I thought about the dog-sized crow, the more convinced I was that it knew me. It was her blood inside that bird.

Today the top of the washing machine was empty. No crows, no memories. While I waited for the washer to begin its cycle, I stood barefoot on the concrete, even though I'd been told that it would allow the cold to enter through the soles of your feet and freeze your uterus and turn you infertile. When Cecilia and I were little, the threat of infertility was scrolled open like a sky above our heads: Don't loop your lips around the nozzle of the drinking fountain, the bacteria will ban you from having babies. Don't sit on a cold bench, wait for the sun to slap it warm, or your womb will become an ice cube. Don't walk around barefoot. Don't sit with your knees apart, or the air will find a door there. Don't get punched in the belly, it will crush your eggs like the ones in those cartons nobody wants to buy. Don't lean over the counter like that, grinding your hips into useless powder. Don't encounter corners. Don't catch what's coming straight at you. Swallow with your mouth shut. Cecilia laughed at all these, saying that grown-ups cared more about our babies than they cared about us. We were just the rinds of future lives, ready to be discarded after our meat was eaten and the seeds sucked out; no one named our scraped scalps or our tanbark scars or our purpling toenails. But I was comforted by these warnings and invested in my destiny. I wanted to fulfill something. Cecilia sat on the frosted bus-stop bench every morning and even ran around the dirt field at school without her shoes or socks on. Ma said only foreigners and country bumpkins went around without their shoes on. But Cecilia didn't believe in a life curated by caution. To her, the future was futile. She did not lie awake for weeks after swallowing a watermelon seed, anticipating a terrible birth, the splitting of herself into seedless halves.

There was a pile of wet laundry heaped on top of the neighboring dryer, knotted together like intestines, and I remembered the time when Cecilia and I were walking by the grocery store. Outside, there was always a man on a plastic stool, a hose clamped in his hands, washing the sidewalk. He was surrounded by buckets of water with gray mops inside them, heavy rags slopped over their rims. I'm not sure what I said, but Cecilia told me those weren't mops in the buckets: the gray rags were rinsed intestines, procured from a former pig. The man transformed when I looked at him again: he was no longer jetting water across the sidewalk but was instead scouring his own hands, erasing any feces. The wet sidewalk shone like the side of a cleaver. I wasn't disarmed by the fact that the mops were actually bodies. What stunned me was the way they were displayed, public and touched by everything. The next time I ate Ama's tripe soup, I thought of those buckets out on the sidewalk, how they were fermented in the air, the sky, my breath, Cecilia's humming. They tasted of too much. I'd rather eat like the crows, delving my beak into the meat and fragmenting its tendons, transferring the flesh directly from the darkness of its carcass to the darkness of my throat. Was it possible, I wondered then, to create a tunnel between two interiors, to shuttle memories from one body into another without ever exposing them to the erosion of fog and sky and eyes?

I slammed the washer shut and went back inside to change the sheet on my plastic-wrapped futon. Ma and Ama were used to water-resistant mattresses from their work at the retirement home, and Ama used to say: *Before you strap a diaper on me, just hang me from the ceiling.*

Ma says: *Whatever you do in life, don't get a job that involves shit. That includes being a veterinarian. It's not the species of shit that's important. It's shit itself. Don't touch it.*

My brother says: *That's why I work with houses. Houses don't shit. Sometimes there's shit inside houses, shit from all species, but as a rule, as a structure, they don't shit.*

Ama says again and again: *You know why people have children? It's a kind of safety net. People think, Now someone will take care of me when I get old! Now I've got someone in my debt! But that's dog shit. I take care of people with children. You think anyone wants to wipe your ass? Like it's gold and just needs a polish? When it's time, don't feel bad about separating me from my life.*

I told Ama I would never hang her from the ceiling, but I'd seen many actors in period dramas hang themselves with silk scarves at the behest of their emperor. When the emperor gifted you a length of white silk, beautiful as milk, it meant that he expected you to handle yourself. You were responsible for authoring the knot, and that terrified me more than death itself. It was the illusion of choice that seemed cruel. It reminded me of the story Ama once told me, how she'd wanted to leave her husband after their first week together but had no other house to return to. Instead of leaving him, she began to knit a red sweater for my mother. For months she labored over this secret project, handling the yarn delicately as if it were an artery. But by the time Ama finished knitting, my mother had outgrown the sweater. Her husband saw this and laughed, saying they would have another child to fill it. Quick as she could, Ama unraveled the sweater back into yarn, but it was too late. She was already pregnant.

I should have knitted myself a scarf, Ama said, laughing. *My neck can't outgrow a noose.*

When I refused to hang her, Ama would just smile and say, *Don't worry, you could do it. You have the capacity to lift me. You have the hands to help me.* She never said explicitly that my species was predator, but the evidence was damning. She trusted me to truss her up.

After wiping down the plastic that protected my futon, I left for work. My brother was gone too, his truck not in its spot beneath the street's only tree. In its bare branches, crows decomposed. Their wings twisted off like leaves, fluttering to the sidewalk. Their beaks softened into faucets of ink. Their feet were so white they were indistinguishable from the sycamore branches they clutched, and I realized their legs were bare bone, their skin flopped off. Walking toward the bus stop, I looked for other trees where crows might be ripening, but there weren't any more trees allowed to live in this part of the city.

At the clinic, I folded.

In the alleyway, crows fled from my face.

The lightbulb died in the laundry room, so I wrapped my hand in a towel to unscrew and replace it.

It was dark when I left, and I locked the front door before realizing I'd forgotten bags of trash behind the receptionist's desk. But the door's glass panel was dull and opaque, as if painted over by an eyelid, as if nothing existed behind it—if I opened the door and stepped inside, there wouldn't even be a floor to girdle my feet—so I turned and left, crossing the parking lot.

At the bus stop was Cecilia. She stood facing the street, unmoving, but I felt she'd been waiting for me. Even from afar, when I first realized there was someone standing in front of the pole, I knew they were waiting for me. My feet delayed my arrival, wanting to wade a little longer in their patience. Their shadow was stretched taut in the frame of the sky. The night was thin enough to puncture with my tongue.

Finally, I stood beside her. Cecilia's posture was so familiar to me: Head jutted slightly forward, eager to examine something. Hand hooking a strand of hair behind her ear. The rounded tip of her ear. The visible tendon snaking up the side of her neck. Even her pinkies were family. She was dressed this time in a dark puffer jacket and jeans, dark boots that made her taller than me. I'd always looked at her from above.

She turned and faced me. *I called the desk to ask about you,* she said, *but the receptionist hung up on me.*

How long have you been waiting? I said.

She smiled, her bottom teeth still as crooked as I remembered, same as mine. We'd thought if we knocked them out of each other's mouths, they would grow back straight, they would never touch tips.

As long as you think, she said. I didn't know what I thought. All my thoughts thrashed in shallow water.

I asked Cecilia why she'd gone to the chiropractor. I knew this was intrusive, and that I could have asked the receptionist, who, despite swearing doctor-patient confidentiality, took pleasure in being reminded that she had access to the private, that she might know more as a stranger than even a patient's closest friends.

Back pain, Cecilia said. *Sometimes my jaw, sometimes my feet. It's the bones, not the muscles.* Ma said the same thing, that her bones took turns hurting. Whenever I complained of a pain, Ma gave me the cure: to make another part of my body hurt even worse, distracting from the original source. If you stub your toe, bash your head into the wall. Play tag with your pain until it's exhausted. Until it flees you.

I clenched my fist until my nails drew blood, concentrating on the pain instead of her face. Then I laughed, suddenly relieved. The sound stuttered out of my mouth like the stop-and-go traffic in the street. We were at a four-way intersection, cars sharking through the night, and I was aware that she could launch herself into the street. Not because she would risk her life, but because she wanted to always be surrounded. She wanted to be the stone dropped into a carp pond.

Bone pain? I said I'd never heard of that. *You're the one who knows everything about bones,* I said, watching her face. I reminded her that a skeleton survives fire. When you're cremated, you turn into a tray of sugar cookies. To become crumbs, you have to be brutally chewed.

Now Cecilia laughed. *When did I say that? I don't think I meant cookies. I don't think we become cookies.*

Her face was flat as a coin in this dark, the green light of a neon sign streaking her left cheek. Her features were familiar, but I was no longer sure if our memories were mutual. Our distance had solidified, and now we could only lean against the barrier of air between us, attempting to touch through a hairless hide of time. She leaned away from me as she spoke, the weight of her body tilting backward, and I thought of the crows that watched me from the dumpster cage, poised to flee, weighing past hurts against present hungers. She spoke, but all her openings—her mouth, her ears, her nostrils—were watching me. A pupil populated each pore, a million eyes welling with sweat.

But wouldn't it be great, she said, *if we died to become tasty treats!*

I tried to laugh and said sweet wasn't the worst way to be. Cecilia said she agreed. She was silent for a second, and I asked her what was causing her bone pain. The bus burst toward us, its horn punching through the traffic. When it jerked to the curb and opened its doors, I hesitated. I turned and extended my hand, as if she were my child and needed help climbing the stairs. It was instinctual, reaching out to her. She stared at the cup of my hand, then bent her head and drooled into it. A jewel jiggled in the center of my palm. A nickel I didn't solicit.

I stared down at it, her heat hammocked in my hand, and Cecilia began to laugh, dragging her wrist across her mouth. We used to scour the pavement for coins, and now she welded them straight to my skin. I shivered and said nothing, turning to board the bus, flicking her eyes off me. A familiar urge filled me, and I knew

I would not wipe the palm of my hand on anything: I would sieve her saliva through my skin, summon it up my own throat. I thought of the handkerchiefs Ama sold at bus stops. Even before I was born, she predicted my uncleanness. From the past, she told me to wipe my palms.

Behind me, Cecilia mounted the steps and entered the aisle, the brightness of the bus flooding the space between us, hardening into armor. I panicked at the thought that we were never going to touch.

Are you going in this direction? I asked her. The bus was half full of ghosts, only the back rows empty, but I didn't want to sit there with her. I needed the floor beneath my feet, assurance we were moving.

Cecilia nodded. *Just to the next stop,* she said, and I had the feeling that she regretted getting on with me, that the fluorescent light had peeled away my falsest face, revealing my predatory one. What did she see? Cecilia was the only one who truly knew what I was capable of, how I could unleash my hands, and she seemed even more resigned now that we were tinned inside a bus, narrowed inside night. I settled into its sway, my belly heavy, the bus unable to writhe out from underneath me. This must be what a predator feels when they trap their prey, cornering them somewhere. Their loping begins to slow, their tongues begin to flood, their skins finally fit. The knowledge that they are nearing, that their stomachs are at stake, results in a renewed burst, a final latching.

Cecilia held onto nothing. When the bus turned, I swung toward her, catching myself with the strap above my head. Bending her knees, Cecilia bobbed a little but didn't shift, and as soon as the bus straightened, I yanked myself away. I was aware of her bones. I knew they were the moon. She privatized her light and heat so that I would feel nothing in our nearness. Next stop, I thought, next stop. Get off.

• • •

You are named Cecilia after the Hong Kong actress, and I am named Seven after the American soda. Ma claims that's all she could drink when she was pregnant with me, 7 Up, and that she had to walk to the 7-Eleven every morning and buy three liters at a time and drink until her piss thickened to syrup, flies orbiting her belly. You were the sweetest when you were inside me, she said, but all babies come out bitter. Screaming and scaring everything. Shocking the dead.

My brother and I think the soda-guzzling is why Ma wears bottom dentures, because her teeth rotted and rolled like dice out of her mouth after so much sweet green, her veins crystallizing too, but she tells us actually, she got bucked off a bus when she was fifteen and a roadside swamp swiped up all her teeth.

You are nine and I am eight. We still own our Mongolian spots, yours blue and mine green. Later, you explain that blue means good and green is mean. Green means someday I'll skin something. It's July when we meet at the laundromat, back when the landlord hasn't yet installed the machines in the side yard. Our mothers leave us alone there for hours while they're next door at the dollar store. We are not allowed at the dollar store because we touch everything, bruise it blue or green.

Because you are nine months older than me, I think of the distance between us as an infant. I dream of peeling the infant like a persimmon, eating the time, teething my way into your tense. Because you're older, you carry yourself like a crown. You remind me of all those concubines on TV, the ones Ma and Ama are always shouting at, who kill their rivals' children or fall in love with another kingdom's emperor or commit some other transgression that culminates in crying or execution or ritual suicide.

You perch atop the tooth-yellow washing machine as if it's a throne, all the machines throbbing like cicada song, and for a second while I watch you, I pretend we're in a scene on TV, a tinfoil lake between us: I'm the soldier who sends you letters written on my dead warhorse's skin, and you are the concubine who belongs to a prince.

We drape our mothers' wet shirts over our heads like wedding veils, looking at our reflections in the glass of the washing machines, pretending they're circular screens and we're being aired as queens. You find a dime on the floor and buy a palm-sized box of powder laundry detergent, pouring it into your mouth and frothing from the jaw like a rabid dog, pretending to have a seizure on the floor just to see if someone might do something. But I am the only one who plays along, who licks the bitterness off your lips.

It's 100 degrees this summer, and the laundromat is the only place in the strip mall with good air-conditioning. Everywhere else, the fans fart with a sense of futility. The kingdom of the laundromat is run by a woman from Hong Kong who holds two cigarettes at a time, one forgotten in her mouth and the other clasped between her knuckles, a rubied ring. We lean back against the machines, feeling them hack like bad lungs— the machines are always broken or nearly broken, and when one of them stutters, the lady walks by and bats it with her broom. Next to you, the smell of my sweat is amplified, and I clamp my arms to my sides, hoping you won't recognize my rodent musk. I smell like the mouse my brother once caught and doused in the sink.

You tell me your mother's a singer, so famous and beloved that fans toss their wedding rings onstage when she sings. A single one of those rings can buy a house in Taipei. She lives in a climate of diamonds, a dazzling downpour. But your mother doesn't look like a singer, with her plastic slippers and no spotlight following her. *It's 'cause she's not on TV right now,* you tell me. When she's on TV, you explain, she's brighter than the blister you get on your thumb from touching a flame. She can undress any song with her tongue. *I have tapes,* you say, inviting me over to watch them. *But what happened to her house in Taipei,* I ask, and you slide away from the washing machine and say it was burnt down. A factory caught fire and your mother's house carried the flame. It sounds like a lie to me, but Ma says factories burn down all the time: once, in LA, the wholesale clothing factory where she worked burned down in the middle of the day and no one knew why. She'd been pregnant and sick with me all week and hadn't gone in that day, and every year on my birthday, she reminds me that I saved her life, and that in a past life, I must have been a starving stray dog she'd fed once.

You've been born to pay me back, she says, and I've wondered what kind of dog I was, if that's why I sometimes foam in my sleep, pearls shivering up my throat. When I tell you that I was once a dog rescued by my mother, that I was born to repay my karmic debt, you say it sounds like a scam. *What's her proof,* you ask, and I say I have none, but neither do you.

The closest I come to seeing your mother on TV is when she's walking back to the laundromat, her permed hair haggling with the sky for some space. She's boxed in by the window, the dusty pane furring her face, and even as she approaches, she stays the same size. Watching her from behind a glass screen, I almost believe she sings a country to sleep.

I see you again at the laundromat the next week, when I'm hauling in my mother's load. Your mother kneels and wrestles a wet sock out of a pant leg, and I decide you're lying. I want to be alone with you, unmediated by mothers. In the meantime, I wait for your mother to speak, but she doesn't say anything, not even when she goes to the wall-mounted machine to exchange her five. I can't imagine her singing. Singers, I believe, should have throats that taper into fingers, or jaws that shine like vases, and their veins should be visible as rivers, full enough to flood. But your mother's exposed throat looks the same as mine, just a little thinner. The hollow at the base of her throat was once a setting for a gem.

When your mother leaves, you climb onto the machine again, saying you like the heave of it beneath you, like the hull of an aircraft, though you've never flown before, and me neither. This time the Hong Kong lady yells at you to get down, your buns will break the machine. You respond in Cantonese, a phrase flicking out like a wing, and I am impressed by this. Cantonese is a language I only hear on TV. Then you look down at me and say you're named after the actress Cecilia, the singer Cecilia, the one your mother used to know. But I think that's a lie: Ma says you can't name your children after real people. She says you can name your children after American actors, because they aren't real, but never after people you know. She never says why, but I think it must have something to do with debts and dogs and everything else. That somehow a name is the blade of your fate, held to your throat all your life.

You shake your head at me, your whole body rattling, and the machine continues munching your mother's clothes. *I think names are nothing,* you say, *I think they're nickels.* The washing machine doesn't take nickels, though your mother always tries.

But I worry someday you'll leave me for the screen, like the Cecilias of your lineage, orbited by eyes, like your mother who left your father. *Because he told her performing is bad for a woman,* you say, *he said only whores sing on TV.*

Horses don't sing anywhere, I say back, and you shake your head. *A horse,* you say, *is a woman with a man inside.* I look down at my flip-flopped feet, the lint between my toes that Ma will pick out later with her pinky nails. I have long suspected I'm a horse. Since last we met, I have dreamt of you as my concubine, wearing only water, while I am the emperor with the daggered beard, filling your belly with melon seeds until you birth me a melon baby. When your belly is ready to be bashed open, you hand me a wooden bat. I tremble, grasping its handle. I feel the air encircling it, pursing into a word I want so badly to speak, to leak.

What do you mean, it's bad to be on TV? I ask. You explain that the more people see you, the more skin is subtracted from you. Enough eyes can recruit knives. If you're watched too often, you might turn into a meatless drumstick. It's not good to be looked at, seen into nothing. But you frown and shrug when you say it, and I know you climb the machines to be seen. I avert my eyes, staring instead at the window in the washer. From now on, I promise myself I will only look at you a little at a time, like nibbling, which Ma doesn't like me to do. If you're going to eat, involve the full mouth, she always tells me, tackle it with your tongue, taste it all the way down. But I don't want you to be eyed too early, projected onto every glass window and screen, singing somewhere too far away to hear, because TV seems to me like a terrible fate: no matter how close the camera zooms in, no matter how famous they make your mouth, you are buried by the screen, lidded by all light. You will never be any nearer to me.

• • •

Cecilia didn't get off at the next stop. She swayed in place and looked down at me. Night evaporated off her back, lining her in a strange light. She faced the back of the bus and I faced the front, the two of us staring at each other, the freckle under her left eye as stark as a fly. Though it didn't move, I knew that I had to slap it dead before it laid eggs in the lake of her pupil. I knew flies fed on rot, and that inside the pouch of her left undereye was a pudding of our past. When she was little, she complained about her undereye purses, convinced they were full of slobber, and when I told her cold spoons could get rid of them, she thought I meant to scoop her eyes from her face, sucking the jelly out of each socket.

Windows flanked us, and night pressed like a pelt to the glass. Cecilia's hair wanted to curtain us completely, swinging between our bodies. Under the fluorescent light, I pretended our pasts were in tandem, but my memories had always outlived hers, even when we were little. The light on the bus reminded me of the golden liquid Cecilia used to bring to school: she carried jar lids trembling with a water that lured slugs. *It's a trap,* she said, *they drown in here.* She would place the traps on the fringe of the dirt field, where some grass still groaned up from the ground. She was careful to place them in the shade of a maple tree: *Darkness and moisture are key for slugs. Their ideal conditions are vaginal.*

When we checked on them in the evening, there were dozens of slugs drowned in the foam, their bodies fizzing into snot. I thought those dishes were filled with her piss. And when I looked down at those slugs solved by her salt, I felt a sudden envy, a hatred illuminating my belly. I wanted to bring those dishes to my lips and slurp them clean, disappear them inside of me. It was unfair that the slugs had lived inside her before dying. I wanted an apology. I wanted a trap laid for me. She coveted what she killed, pouring out each dish of slugs into a hole in the field, covering it with dirt, stranding me outside her grief. *Their funerals should last just as long as their lives,* she said. That need for symmetry again. Though I tried to match her passion for slaughter, all I could do was stew in my resentment. She emptied the jar lids as if she were watering a beloved, and she was so excited to count her casualties that she lied about needing to go to the bathroom just to check on the lids. *Look,* she said, tugging me into a crouch. She plucked two slugs and lifted them to her ears. *How do I look? These are babies, so dainty. The ones that died before they were grownups. That means we're causing an extinction. After this, there will be no more generations. These are the last. Should I get my ears pierced and wear them as earrings? In honor of their species?* I stepped forward and flicked the babies away like boogers, splattering them onto the grass. They hadn't earned her earlobes. Why were the dead allowed to dangle from her, to occupy her holes, while the living had to keep their distance?

Later I learned that Cecilia's dishes were likely filled with beer, and that the slugs were attracted to the smell of its yeast.

Do you still hate slugs? I asked her. We rocked back and forth as the bus turned up a hill. The sleeves of her jacket bulged as she shifted, the material shiny and wet as a skinned lip.

She smiled. *I don't hate slugs,* Cecilia said, *I've always loved them.*

I swallowed, remembering how happy she'd been counting those slugs. She loved them because she was responsible for their deaths. Her killing was care, and she pledged her loyalty to their afterlives, ensuring they were buried together, never to be lonely.

Cecilia said, *Slugs are male and female. They fertilize their own eggs. Every slug comes from a single slug. Every slug belongs to only one. I like that symmetry.*

I used to wish she could be my mother or my daughter. That we could have come from one another. That we would never have to split our ownership with anyone. I made her swear she'd name her child after me, and I'd name mine after her. We would both make a chain of repeating names. In every generation, there'd be a Cecilia and a Seven, swapping our genes between them. Next generation, there would be a Cecilia with my blood and a Seven with her bones. It excited me, the idea of a Cecilia who descended from me, dripped from me, but Cecilia said she didn't like the name Seven.

I don't think anything should belong to only one, I said.

Cecilia was still smiling. *I'm just saying, it would uncomplicate things,* she said.

We were technically slugs, I told her, since both of us only came from one person, our mother.

Cecilia was laughing now. *Remember how you used to think boys gave birth to boys and girls gave birth to girls?* She brushed by the words, not really saying them, the way people adjust something on a shelf without taking it out, not wanting to excavate anything. Her ability to skim memories meant they hadn't settled inside her, hadn't become her marrow. We were asymmetrical.

I thought about how I had reasoned: *A guava tree makes guavas, a kumquat tree makes kumquats. My mother made me, my father made my brother. A guava tree doesn't make kumquats, a kumquat tree doesn't make guavas.* What lived in me later, though, was her reaction, not my own confusion: Cecilia looked at me, gripping my wrist and twisting. *You know nothing,* she said. *You need me to fill you. You're completely seedless.* I told her I liked seedless fruit, I liked not having to tongue-wrestle flesh and spit out shards. She laughed and said my brother came out of my mother, same as me. This seemed illogical to me, like opening a watermelon and finding its flesh was made of fish, and for weeks I didn't believe her. But even when I didn't believe the things she said, her words wafted through me. My horror was a hallway, and she was at both ends of it, corralling me in, cornering me into an understanding. Without her, I was empty of horror, unoccupied by anything. Without her, I wasn't haunted, which Ma said was just another word for full. When your body is home to more than just your body, you are turning into a whole.

Yes, I said to Cecilia, *I remember that.* My words fluttered across her shoulders without settling, and she kept smiling. *I miss when we were kids,* she said, and I almost hated her for herding all our memories into the past, into the passive.

Then she shifted her weight between her feet, rolling her neck. She said that because of her back pain, it would be better for her to sit down, though not for too long. The bus rattled, and we neared the stop where Ama and I used to get off every weekend, where the grocery store lived with its buckets of intestines, where all the best dumpsters hung out.

I led her toward the unoccupied part of the bus, toward the back rows, the seats glinting with other people's sweat. Soda-can tabs shivered like scales on the floor. Ma always warned me that perverts loved little girls sitting in the backmost rows, but I sat down next to the window in the last row and waited to see which seat Cecilia would take, if she would choose the one nearest me.

She sat down in the center of the back row, one empty seat between us. The bus lurched away from the grocery store, and we rode in silence until it stopped again. Beside me, Cecilia tilted her head forward, her chin drilling into her chest, probably performing some neck exercise the chiropractor had recommended. I stared out the window, seeing nothing, the night thickening.

Did you have an injury? I asked, without turning to face her. Cecilia said no, her chin still pecking her chest.

I think it's hereditary, she said, then paused. *Maybe I get it from you.*

I told her I'd never had back pain. *Then maybe you'll get it from me,* she said, and in the window reflection, I saw her shrug one shoulder at a time, hissing as she exhaled.

Stack your ache on top of my skull, I wanted to say, let me eat your bones clean. How much lighter you'll feel then, what relief.

I tried looking out the window instead of at her reflection, though the darkness was no distraction.

Rows ahead of us, a man and a woman half stood from their seats, ready to slink toward the doors at the next stop. The bus was emptying like a nosebleed, clots of people sliding by the windows, but Cecilia hadn't told me yet where she was going. Back when she was a kid, she'd lived in the other direction, on the left side of the sky, closer to the cleft hill we called the Buttcrack.

Are you following me? I asked, trying to sound light. But I realized I'd missed my stop long ago, which meant that technically, I was now following her.

Cecilia didn't answer, and her neck rippled in the watery reflection of my window, the arc of her throat filling in for the night. Sweat slimed my palms, slugs of it crawling down my spine. How much further, I wondered, was she going to take me. Cecilia's skull was a satellite, orbiting her neck as she did her exercise. The empty seat between us shimmered with a silhouette, sequins of our heat embellishing the air. In the window's reflection, her head untethered from her neck and began to orbit both of us. My head fizzed with dizziness until I could no longer tell whether the bus was moving or mourning, nearing or disappearing.

• • •

My name lives only in your mouth. It isn't acclimated to any other conditions, doesn't dabble in any other dark. Your tongue basks in the right acidity. Your bacteria cultivate my climate. Your teeth gnash the syllables of my name into silt. Your cheeks pouch with my excrement. In return, my mouth pits the moon and spits its seed onto your face: it lives there today as the mole under your left eye. That eye has a habit of wandering. Sometimes it ferments in the dish of beer where hundreds of slugs undrape. Sometimes I find it's a fly, forever tethered to your lower lip. It startles when you speak and flees to me, touching down on my tongue and feasting on its meat. I wonder what it sees at the threshold of my hunger.

The name *Cecilia* means "blind to one's own beauty." It comes from Latin. We live inside languages we don't know. I confuse the words *sea* and *see, seen* and *scene*. When I spot you on the playground before school, straddling the top of the jungle gym, grinding your crotch against the cold metal bars without any worries of future infertility, I hold my breath, stranded by the sight of you. Crows gather overhead and unload their droppings into our palms, warming our hands. It makes me wonder what it would be like to stand directly beneath you, filtering everything you pour into me. I'm happy to be your sieve, for your purest form to pass through me. In class, when you raise your hand to ask permission for a bathroom pass, I do the same. Though the teacher scolds us and says we can only go one at a time, that there's no way our bladders are synced like clocks, I hear a ticking sound deep in my belly and know that it's your baby.

I don't know what I pee out of. If it's a rose or a nose or a teakettle spout or a water fountain or a punctured pipe or a horse's mouth. My pee changes direction depending on the angle of my squat or how I sit on the rim of the toilet, sometimes scurrying down my knees and sometimes scattering on the floor or spraying the back of my pants if I don't pull them all the way to my ankles. Whatever I pee out of, it must have a million settings.

Ever since you revealed to me that my brother holds his penis when he pees, my hands begin to bloat with longing, swelling with their own emptiness. As consolation,

I bring a guava into the bathroom and squeeze it like an udder, tightening my fist until it evicts a canine-shaped seed.

I am jealous that you have pubic hair and I don't. You say it's because I don't eat meat, I only eat fish. But that isn't true: I recount to you the KFC drumstick I shared with Ma and Ama, who took turns eating the skin and the bones.

I know you have pubic hair because you show me: in the bathroom stall at recess, you unhook your pants from your hips and tug them down and point and say look, *Look, lashes.* You whisper that last night a pubic hair, a pinky-length one, got up your butt. You didn't know they could get in there, you say, but you just felt something stuck. Like a loose tooth, it kept bothering you. So finally you pulled it out, and it was a single hair with globs of shit pearling it. *Just like going fishing,* you say, laughing.

You invent a secret code to indicate when there is a hair inside you, and in which hole. One is phrased with two hooked fingers in a *J,* and the other is a left fist. I am thrilled that you want me to be privy to this information, to be part of this wordless intimacy, and I mirror every hand signal back at you, showing my solidarity. I flash the signals at you so often that you start to become wary.

No, I insist, it happens to me too, all the time, a hair went fishing inside me, and when I tugged it out, it was an earthworm with a face like mine. You say you know

I'm lying, it feels nothing like an earthworm. You ask me what hole I pulled it from.

The only one, I say.

The only one? you say, laughing. You say there are three, three holes, and I don't believe you. The love-bird at home has one hole for droppings, and Ma says it might someday lay eggs out of the same one. I'm afraid for the lovebird because I don't understand how an egg can fit inside its belly, but Ma says it will lay a little egg, not a chicken egg. *It will experience a pain of its own proportions,* she says, *don't worry about it exploding.*

Ma teaches me how to palpate the lovebird's pelvis to predict whether it will lay eggs. I think this is unnecessary; if it's got an opening, a baby will come out of it. But Ama says that's not true, all birds have one hole, no matter if they lay eggs or don't. To mate, they rub their holes together. But how is that possible? A hole is an absence, and two absences can't touch. A doorway can't fill another doorway. If I press the mouths of two cups together, both remain empty. Something must enter the bird to put the baby inside. Or can you make a baby the way you start a fire with friction, raising a flame from nothing, filling your belly with smoke? But even then, something must enter to put out the fire. Ama shakes her head and says I lack creativity, that not everything exists to be entered, to be made useful. A hole, like all empty space, is pure potential. Filling it with something, however satisfying, erases its infinite possibilities. *It's better for your body to be empty,* Ama says, *to be purposeless. To be free.*

One hole, I repeat to you, *we have one hole.* Like the soft-serve machine at Hometown Buffet. There's a lever above the nozzle, and depending on how low you pull it, the nozzle will squeeze out a vanilla swirl, a chocolate swirl, or a braided vanilla-and-chocolate swirl. When I explain this to you, you laugh and say it's not one nozzle. We don't flick like a switch.

To ensure the lovebird isn't egg bound, I feel for the fork of its pelvic bones and measure the width of the crevice. It gives me a sense of vertigo, the dip of emptiness between hip bones. Ama says it will never lay anything, since it has no mate to endure, but Ma says you just have to wait: eventually, it will lay an egg out of sheer loneliness. The lovebird nips my knuckles, and I release it back into the cage on top of the TV. I've been taught how to probe the lovebird's pelvis, how to comb the forest of its bones, but I don't know how many holes I own. *Three,* you tell me, three. I know the one that pickles liquid, the one that cuffs the sleeves of my guts, but I don't know the third one. The one that cries open for cold air, that lets in death. You say it's a swinging door, opening one way for men and opening the other way for babies, and I pray for its hinges to rust, to keep itself shut. *But I'd open it for you,* I say. If you asked me to, I would reach inside myself and reserve the space under your name. Shaking your head, you say I'm too selfless, that I should try slipping a finger inside and keeping it there until I no longer feel its presence. You say there is nothing more noble than being full of ourselves.

In class, I part my legs and slither one hand into my waistband, shrouded by the shadow of my desk. Boys do it too, standing in the lunch line with their hands grafted to the front of their pants. But Ma catches me doing it at home on the sofa and says I'd better sit with my legs shut or she'll cut off my kneecaps and boil them into soup.

At night, when I can't sleep, I slip both hands into my underwear. It's as necessary for sleep as shutting my eyes. It's ritual, like putting your hand over your heart for the pledge of allegiance, except I don't remember all the words, I just repeat, *undergod, undergod, undergod,* the only words I never forget, because my mother says god is underground, god is your dead family saying I'm hungry.

I decide it's okay to touch myself as long as I assign each part of my body a different species. My hands are salamanders, cold blooded, and they need to sleep inside the heat of my crotch to survive the night. Outside of me, they die. I tuck my sheets in tight. My heart is a rodent, which is why it eats itself. And my legs are eels, the kind with two sets of jaws stacked like bracelets, allowing them to eat large prey. I eat everything twice, swallowing in succession. Again and again and again.

In my dreams, I have a penis. It's a beloved green slug with three eyeballs that opal its tip. Standing at the prow of a tinfoil fishing boat, the same one my agong steered, I wring out the slug with both hands, a slurry of tinier slugs dribbling out of its tip, plinking into the water like tongues. Your mouth is the sea, and I know that you drink me because the boat bobs like a throat beneath my feet, beneath my dreams.

For weeks you've been saying you're going to invite me over to watch your mother on TV, but I think you are afraid to lead a predator to the nest. Instead, I invite you to my house, where the TV blinks like an animal's eyes in the night. Where every touch is taxed. You try to feed your fingertip to the lovebird, wedging it between the bars of the cage, juicing it bloodless. *They don't eat meat,* I say, *only seed.* You tell me that all lovebirds have to live as a pair or else they die of loneliness. In that cage on top of the TV, it doesn't even have a mirror. You wad a KFC napkin into a bird and draw it a face, your face. But when you slide it between the bars of the cage, the lovebird shreds it to ash, scatters it on the floor. It's defending its solitude, the territory of its sorrow. It registers even its fallen feathers as intruders. *Maybe you are its mate,* you say, *maybe it thinks you're half of it.*

But I am not that kind, I want to say. I am not prey. When I burrow my fingertip between the bars of the cage, it flinches and flees to the opposite side, gripping the metal until it rusts. Out of everyone in my family, the lovebird fears my hands the most, only allowing me to empty its dish of sunflower seeds. Only permitting utility.

It is the first time you disappoint me: the lovebird understands more than you do. It sees the proof of my predation. It records the root of my movements, makes a log of my longings. It sings most when I'm not home. Ama says it is born in me to hurt things, that when I was a baby I gnawed through my own umbilical cord despite my toothless jaw, tucking the cord between my legs like a tail, chasing the light around the room, swooning into a row of scalpels. The signs are in my beak-like forefingers, in the reckless swing of my earlobes, in the four cowlicks on my scalp, more than anyone else in my family, the ones that correspond to the rungs of my temper, multiplying like rings in water. In its cage on top of the TV, the lovebird watches me, head turned to the side. It freezes when I move. It pretends to be you.

• • •

You say you are interested in my ama. You are interested in her ability to season every story with spite or lace up its endings with laughter. I wish you would say: Tell me a story about the hunters you come from. I would tell you.

Ama says three things killed her: first was marriage, which she told me I should never do, because men are like those inedible mushrooms that grow in people's yards, they're bright as pork fat and shiny as doorknobs but will actually cause vomiting until death if you accept them into yourself, plus their pricks roam the earth and impregnate everything, because even when men are penniless they spend themselves inside other women; the second was having children, which resulted in varicose veins in her vulva and a torn asshole, which resulted in lifelong constipation that fills her bowels with gas and hardens her belly into a buoy, which she says is actually useful because none of us ever learned how to swim and now she floats without trying; and the third was the war. Which war, I ask her, but she says she doesn't remember, only that the babies—she was one of them—were evacuated by their mothers, thrown into wells while planes prowled overhead. Decades later, she was ladled out of a neighboring city's toilet. *They put me straight to work cleaning it,* she says, *can you believe it. You don't ask a human to wipe the place they've just popped out of!*

Ama says she remembers everything about being a baby, about being thrown down a well and perching her breath on the stone rim of it, about nursing from a pig's teat so she could eat the breast afterward, about licking the wall of the well and how sweet it was, exactly like the strawberry soft-serve at Hometown Buffet, where she goes every Sunday for the Senior Special, where we sit together in a plastic booth and eat slices of honeyed ham and six courses of green Jell-O from the same plate. My brother says it's impossible to remember things from when you were a baby, because your brain hasn't yet been hardboiled and is still runny inside the skull, which is why you can't shake babies, because otherwise the whites of their minds dribble out of their ears, but Ama says she can. She narrates with knives, etching shapes into the linoleum table with her cutlery, double-tracing circles to show me the opening of the well, the water where she was wombed.

She draws a horizon on the table and says *lineage* is actually pronounced *leanage,* as in who we lean on, who we lean into—all the women in our family stand shoulder to shoulder, leaning on each other, not vertical but horizontal. A horizon of mothers. You can turn in any direction and still be facing one another. It makes punching each other easier, in cases when you seek vengeance, and you can lend each other clothes and frozen sheets of dough without having to strain upward. There are no lines in our family, only leans. My mother and her mother on either side of me, leaning like crooked teeth. One teaches me how to gnaw myself free, the other tells me never to leave.

When we're done eating Jell-O, Ama takes me around to the back of the restaurant and boosts me into the dumpster. Look for aluminum, she says, the pure stuff. I collect soda-can tabs in my mouth and spit them out, pretend I have silver teeth like Ama, a molar that's a moon. Anything that shines I lift from the dumpster and fling into her trolley. My brother has just joined the Boy Scouts, and every week, the Boy Scout who collects the most recyclables wins a prize. While the trolley fills up, Ama says you never know what you might end up carrying, like how she gave birth to my oldest aunt without even noticing she was pregnant, because her belly was so taut with gas from her perpetual constipation that she mistook my aunt for the latest of her farts. Ama says she gave birth to her on the beach. After spotting Venus in the sky one morning, Ama walked all the way from her house to the shore, trying to get close enough to touch that other planet. *I always thought I'd be a good astronaut,* Ama says, *because you can't pee in space. It'll float away and hit someone in the face. And I'm very good at holding it in.* But she was so distracted by her celestial mission that she didn't notice the heaviness descending from her body. She caught my aunt in a grocery bag and carried her home in it, swinging the infant from her elbow, and when she arrived, she held a hand mirror between her legs and stitched herself up. *Stitches all the way to the asshole!* she says. *Daughters and their big heads!*

That's completely impossible, my brother says, *and also disgusting.* I never ask Ama to show me proof, to show me a scar or the floss she used, but I believe her, because my aunt ended up suffocating herself with a knotted grocery bag and getting cremated on a weekend. Ma says she was a troubled sister, that she had no shadow and no husband, but Ama told me she must have remembered how she was born, and she must have wanted to do it again, to be carried home in a plastic bag and held for the first time, to open her mouth only for milk, never air. It doesn't matter how she died, because she resurrected forty-nine days later as a baby with a different name and a different face, and when I point her out on TV, a miracle infant nursed fat by raccoons in a parking lot, Ama says, *At least her head doesn't look so huge on screen.* She's nocturnal now, my aunt, and at the dumpsters I leave her a plastic bag full of chicken bones that chatter her name.

After we're done snagging aluminum, Ama asks me if I know why people pay money for metal, why we love the shine of things, silver watches and gilded coins and garnets like clotted blood. I say I don't know, and Ama says it's because of water. Long ago, when we were all babies, when we had no word for water, we wandered around and looked for something to slot into that space. We wanted a lid for our mouths. Those of us who survived were sensitive to shine. We learned to see the knife-light of water on some distant horizon and drifted toward it and lived. Ama walks me across the parking lot toward the bus, pausing to spit on the blacktop, a fist of spittle that glitters at my feet like ruined crystals. *There,* she says, *that's the water we walk toward. All the words we know.* Inside her spatter I see peppered glass, I see seeds of salt, I see the emerald droplets of the Jell-O we spooned up together, I see bits of fatty ham like quartz, I see her name, I see myself refracted in her mouth. Her spit swallows the light, warps it into glue, into amber, the kind used to preserve bugs and bone. I want to be fossilized in it, drag my feet into it, pedestal myself. But Ama is saying hurry up, we're going to miss the bus, so I push the trolley and she pulls it and the bus curves toward us, rattling like a soup can. On the ride home, we pass the same billboard over and over again, printed with the face of a personal injury lawyer who promises we'll soon be reimbursed. Ama laughs and says, *How do you reimburse an injury? By pumping your blood into the person you've cut? Ripping out your hip*

bone to replace theirs? Killing a healthy animal and swap-
ping their skin with it?

When we get home, Ama uses the end of her cane
to batter the cans into flat discs, which I kick down the
street like hockey pucks, shouting *Goal!* when I strike a
tree and concuss its leaves. The cane is wrapped in neon
duct tape so she can walk around at night and not get hit
by cars, deer, or aliens. Ma says it's dangerous to walk
at night, but Ama says it's actually safer. In the daytime,
the sun stalks her. It gropes her everywhere she's got
skin, shading it in. This doesn't make sense to me—isn't
it the sun that gives you light and the night that lathers
you in shadow? But Ama says no, it's the opposite, and
at least there's no sunlight when you're dead and stuck
in an urn, and you can pale in peace.

Since as long as Ama has been alive, we've lived near
airports. The airplanes fly low, taking off or landing.
None of the planes ever combust midair, not even when
I pray for fireworks. Sometimes I wear earplugs made
from tissues or wet cotton balls. Ama's the only one who
never once ducked or flinched or moaned when an airplane skimmed across the water of the sky, who never
once complained about the noise at night, the red flickering lights. My brother says it's because she's probably
deaf and doesn't even know what's going over her own
head, but I once saw Ama locate a fly on my kneecap and
slap it dead in her sleep, reaching all the way across her
mattress to enter my airspace. *I'm not scared,* Ama says
about the planes: she says she's used to the sound, and

wouldn't it be nice if they flew a little lower so we could latch onto their legs?

My second aunt almost died that way: when she was little, she tried to leap from the roof of a neighbor's house onto another neighbor's grape arbor, dreaming of swinging from the vines like a cartoon, but children, my ama says, weigh more than grapes, and the vines were too weak. She broke both legs and was bedridden, the bones dissolving into milk and calcifying in new shapes. After that, Ama says, she walked like a man. Her new bones were for a boy much older than her. *Just like your bones,* she says, when I sit with my legs apart and explain they naturally fall that way. Even when I magnetize my knees, they hinge open again like the door in our house that never stays shut, which my brother blames on a demon made of dust. *Don't ever eat grapes,* Ama tells me, and I agree, even though I want a boyhood for my bones.

My brother says that's a sign of senility, her blaming the grapes and not my aunt, but I say it's memory. I ask Ama if I'll ever remember my own infant memories— all I know is that Ama pushed me around in her trolley at night, that she gave me my first solid food, a strip of salted fish I apparently choked on, which is why my throat still stalls on certain words, like *water.* She tells me that it's possible, but she doesn't tell me how.

That night, when Ama is asleep on the mattress beside me, I stand up in the dark and try to whisk my brain back to water, jumping up and down to juice it, lobbing myself at the wall so my mind will shatter like a melon.

Ama wakes up and reaches over and grabs my ankle and tells me to stop, stop, but I toss myself onto the ground and rattle my head, remembering my oldest aunt and the way she drowned in air, her mouth filling with pure fury, and Ama picks me up and says *A well, a well, hurry,* and in her arms I remember when she lolled out of me like a tongue, when I sheared her cord between my legs and dropped her into the sweetest water, when I told her to wait, just wait, my baby, I'll come back for you so soon.

• • •

You say babies are born floating, and that's why there are umbilical cords attached to them. You're supposed to hold onto their balloon strings and reel them down and fill their bellies with slugs so that they'll be heavy enough to sit on their own asses.

I tell you a story that Ma told me, about how her sixth older sister, the one born right before her, was given away to another family. *Given away,* Ma says to me, *not sold, because to sell something implies value, implies demand. That's the way everyone was,* she says: *Zhong nan qing nu. Heavy son light daughter.*

You say, *Isn't it better to be light? Born weightless and with a helium heart, balloon strings tethering us to our mothers' wrists?* But I tell you that sometimes, at night, Ma says she wonders what happened to that sister, wonders every time she sees someone with her face. Night is when she tells stories, because that way, they don't have to adapt to light. They can remain the same as they were inside her body. There are some stories you can't tell during the day, because they've lived so long in the dark of your belly that they can't ever survive the light outside. But at night, stories can travel from dark to dark without having to grow eyes.

You nod and say you wish there were a girl in the world with your face, an intimate stranger. *Maybe you're my sister,* you say, and laugh. But I say it's impossible, because Ma had varicose veins in her vulva that were caused by her pregnancy with me, and my name is still written in those veins.

You say there's an easy way to find Ma's missing sister: just read the mouths of strangers. Since the sister never suckled from my ama's breast, you say that her mouth must still be gaping for its missing shape. Mouthing for the nipple is our first word, you explain to me, which is why the word for mother is so similar in all languages. Nipples are etymology. Our first word is thirst. If I spot a woman whose mouth is the shape of a nipple, if she suckles on her thumb and car exhaust pipes, she must be Ma's missing jiejie. But I shiver to think of nipples: I remember the time we walked home from school and needed to pee and couldn't go behind trees because our mothers told us to keep our waistbands cinched to the skin at all times. We had to use the toilets in the locker room at the YMCA, and there was a woman inside, changing alone, a white towel warping her waist. Her nipples looked so different from mine—darker and larger and dimensional—that at first I didn't know what they were. Maybe a second set of eyes about to swivel in my direction, incriminating my gaze. I turned from her. My first thought was that there was no relation between our bodies, not even on the level of species. I would float away, and she would stay anchored to this earth.

In front of the heavy bathroom door, you saw me looking at her and laughed, saying that someday we'd have breasts. But I couldn't believe you, couldn't believe that we could grow any more limbs than the ones we owned now, that we could spontaneously spawn more shadows. The idea of growing breasts was as foreign to me as sprouting a dozen heads or holes in our palms. When you changed in the locker room at school, I tried to meet the gaze of your nipples, but they were sheathed in fabric. I treasured the pane of your chest, flatter even than mine, so flat that it sometimes bowled: a bowl I wanted to lap clean and ring, a bowl that bathed your heart. You kept talking about the woman's breasts: *Don't you remember sucking on those? I do. My first memory is of biting off a bulb of blood. Her skin tasted like a soda can in the sun.*

I don't want to tell you that I was never breastfed, that breasts are strangers to me: I was a formula baby. Ma had to work, her breastmilk wetting her uniform shirt until it tore like a paper bag. Ama whisked the formula and fed it to me. She changed my diapers too, and sometimes, when the commercials are on, she leans in close and whispers that once, when she was changing my diaper, my intestines unraveled from my asshole, flopping onto the table like fish guts. They were opaline and so long, much longer than the cable behind the TV, twice as long as a child's jump rope. *I was so shocked,* she tells me, *that I just started stuffing them back inside you! Without a word!*

No one knows this happened but you and me, Ama says. *Don't tell anyone else.* But I tell you, only you, that my intestines must be loose inside me, ribboning around like jellyfish. And you laugh and say I must have unspooled them so my ma and ama would have a string to hold onto. I must have been so afraid of floating away. I must want to be knotted to something. You curl your fingers into a fist, and I imagine squatting over it, I imagine your hands scuffling inside my belly, grasping my guts. Holding me the way I want.

At school, whenever it's a girl's birthday, all her friends bring her balloons and tie them to the shoulder straps or handle of her backpack, mylar balloons wearing spacesuits or polka dots, some transparent and filled with smaller neon balloons, some in the shape of hearts, some sunflowers, some bright with tinsel and streamers, some tiered like birthday cakes, some that sing like Tweety when you punch them hard enough, some so big they swivel like globes, the girl tethered to her sky by dozens of rubber vertebrae, gifted her own gravity. Some girls can't even fit their backpacks through the doorway and have to leave the balloons outside, knotted to textbooks or weights wrapped in cellophane. For a whole day, some girls are accompanied by a stratosphere of silver, tugging the moon along on a leash, dozens of plump planets bumping asses above their heads.

When it's my birthday, you bring me a single balloon. Though it's lonely, tethered to my backpack with cooking twine and not with glossy ribbon, the kind of twine that's for knotting raw meat, though it's not a balloon you would buy at the counter of Party City, where the man stands in front of cartoons and clouds and clowns, hooking the balloon's mouth around the nozzle and filling it with helium, though it's just a red rubber balloon you get in a thirty-pack at the dollar store, and it smells like the glove of a dentist as he palpates your gums and glugs your blood, it's still my planet. I was born where your mouth met its mouth.

Taut with your breath, its skin is the membrane of an egg, veined and naked, hoarding a heartbeat. Inside it, your face unfurls, squirming to be born. The balloon does not float, does not fly, does not overthrow the crows. Instead of helium, it is filled with your morning breath. I love it better for its stench, and I carry the balloon under my shirt, soothing it like a belly. The other girls laugh because it drags on the ground as I walk around, gathering gravel and a skirt of dust, and at lunch, you take the teacher's scissors and snip the twine, unable to weather their watching, their laughter. But they don't know how I'm humbled by this bag of your breath, this bladder of stifled wind, how I stroke the rubber skin until it glows with sweat, how I want to prick it open with my pinky nails and spoon out your air like a stew. In the bathroom, you strangle the balloon with your knees and raise your stolen scissors, ready to gut it open, but I grab your wrist. I refuse to let you pop the moon. Until today, I didn't know you were capable of shame. I want to be the cause of it, so I tuck the balloon under my armpit and carry it like a cyst, pretending it's grown out of me. Later, I will tote it home and care for it, feed it bits of lint. I will raise your shame as my own.

For days I imagine your mouth on the balloon's puckered belly button, blowing it full. Inside is a perfume of everything you've ever digested, of the bacteria rugging your tongue in the mornings, of the last song you sang to yourself, of the last time you said my name. The heaviness of your breath is more precious to me than flight. When I hold the red balloon to the sun, it remains as opaque as a blood clot, and I strategize how to swallow it whole and herd it toward my heart.

Though you've snipped it free, I keep the string in my pocket. The twine cord yanks me, thrusts me through hallways, lugs my spine to the right and to the left. When they say *infertile*, do they mean your babies won't be born floating? That your babies will drag on the ground, filled with your breath? If someday we become infertile, will we still be allowed balloons and their blood-warm cords? What will loosen the knots of our need?

The balloon deflates within a day, and my brother laughs and says it looks like a ball sack. It wrinkles and shrivels, the rubber skin overripening, loosening its grip around your breath, and I mourn the air it sheds. I wish

I'd inhaled the balloon's air in the bathroom, the way the boys steal the girls' birthday balloons, slitting their skins to breathe in the helium. I can't imagine what my voice would sound like if your breath were powering it. My voice would become yours, lower and full of holes, a latticed voice that the past pokes through.

You walk with your eyes to the ground. We want a lid for our mouths. I say only the sky will do, and you say to look for a soda can. Anything silver will satisfy. On the benches at school, we play a game all the girls play: we rock the soda can tab back and forth until it snaps off. Each time we press the tab forward or fold it back, watching it flick like a tongue, we recite a letter of the alphabet. When the tab breaks off, the letter you land on is the first letter of the first name of the boy you will marry. All the girls gather to this game. You and I play. I pray as I pinch the tab between my thumb and forefinger, pray as I yank: *C, C, C.* I twist too hard, and the tab snaps off at *A.* The girls laugh, and you do too. *You must really like someone whose name begins with an early letter,* they say, singing the names within reach, and in my mind I repeat *C, C, C,* a sea of *C*'s tipping, leaning back into boats, sailing me toward the nameless place where I am known.

We were on the freeway now, between cities. Between memories. In the center of the back row, Cecilia finished rotating her head like a plucked bird on a spit, the grease of her sweat dripping into her lap. Now she sat still, her back straight. The seat between us was still empty, its plastic drenched in heat, beaded with some other country's humidity. I watched her in the reflection of the window, pretending to be looking out at the freeway. But it was her silhouette that occupied me, the egg made of shadow that squeezed out of her mouth, our silence squirming inside its shell.

The night was too thick to interpret, the city censored by the cinder-block walls of the freeway, but I still recognized this direction. We were headed toward the casino where Ma and Ama used to go on their birthdays. Toward Nickel City, where Cecilia and I once spent her birthday. Though nickels were useless at the laundromat, they were the primary currency of Nickel City, the capital of our hearts, the city we decided to move to when we grew up. We thought anything that contained the word *city* was an actual city, one governed by our desires, accommodating our bladders. When I asked how we would move there, Cecilia said we could hollow our future tits into boats, so we better grow them soon.

At Nickel City, we played pinball on machines with twinging needles, we played Skee-Ball and plugged the holes with our fists, we slid on our asses across the air hockey tables. We spent our sweat and saliva liberally. Cecilia had the voice of a seagull too far from land, screaming for a shore. Ma complained about having to exchange a dollar for a fistful of nickels, like ruining an egg by crumbling its shell into the yolk.

But the game Cecilia loved best involved no machine, just the slot between two knuckles. It was a game she had learned from the boys, who played it on their desks at school: one boy laid his fist flat on a surface, as if he were knocking on a door, and the other boys flicked a penny as hard as they could, bouncing it off the first boy's knuckles. Whoever flays the most skin wins the game. At Nickel City, I squatted on the green carpet and propped my fist on the floor while Cecilia flicked the nickel into my knuckles. It pinged off the middle knuckle of my left hand. My blood squeezed out as slime. Cecilia bent her head to the carpet and picked up the stray slugs of my blood, dangling them from her fingertips, collecting them in her palm, taking them home to drown.

My favorite game was sitting on the plastic saddle of the stationary motorcycle. You pressed a button near the stirrup that selected one of six settings, and I chose the white-sanded beach. The plastic saddle buzzed my name again and again, humming and heating between my legs, its voice spurring my veins, charging the place where I peed until my bladder boiled over and I pissed on the seat a little. Cecilia laughed as I wiped the motorcycle with my sleeve, erasing any trace of my glistening, but when I bent to smell the plastic, it still stank. Even after the screen turned black, I swayed the motorcycle from side to side, imagining its wheels slicing the sea from the shore, imagining Cecilia sewn flat on the sand: I'd avenge my split knuckles by mowing her into meat, and crows would descend to pluck at her pixels, subtracting her color by color.

On the bus, every window broadcast her face. Cecilia turned to the window, our eyes meeting in reflection. She didn't speak. Looking at her reflection was like skimming a muscular river with my finger, knowing that my own hunger lurked in the depths. When I turned to look at her for real, her eyes were glazed and distant, contemplating the night outside, and I was pained to see that something else occupied her. She demanded an entire world, while I could be sustained solely by the sight of her.

Not wanting her to sense this difference between us, I turned back to the window: outside, the night was thick with crows, a dark composed of many bodies. The freeway was mostly empty. Only a few headlights hung in the air before disappearing, flitting toward other cities.

Cecilia was waiting. Though her eyes in the window were a reflection, I was certain that they were hovering outside the bus, that her gaze was coming through the pane. When I whipped my head around to look at her, they were located on her face. Yet the feeling did not fade: her eyes were the night's. They looked in, lapping my chin.

I pressed my fingertips to her reflection and pried at her eyes, hoping to disturb her, but the face in the window was cold and smooth and glass. Then suddenly my hand flung itself off the pane. The bus swerved across two lanes, its headlights leering to the left, Cecilia thrashing in her seat. Three rows ahead of us, a woman in a wig was thrown sideways into the aisle, her hair lagging a second behind her. Someone cursed their mother. The fluorescent light swung and splattered the windows.

Dislocated from its lane, the bus bailed to the right, about to roll onto its back and bare its belly. I gripped the edge of the seat with both hands and veered into the empty seat beside Cecilia, my shoulder shunting into hers. The sleeve of her puffy jacket crinkled against me, and the sheer heat of her body reminded me of one recess when we were sharing a bag of pretzels we'd found on the ground. Cecilia stood up to chase the crows that were passing a hot dog from beak to beak, and I reached into the bag for another pretzel. When I slotted it into my mouth, I sensed immediately that something was wrong: the pretzel was warm and wet and disintegrating like a wad of tissue. Too late, I realized that it was one of the pretzels Cecilia had put it in her mouth and spat out again, soggy and the same temperature as her tongue: she only liked the salt, she said, and so she suckled until the crystals dissolved. Then she spat the pretzel out whole. Though I should have cast it out of my mouth—only birds regurgitated to feed each other—I harbored it in my cheek, mushing it against my gums, tasting it across many days. The knowledge that I'd put something in my mouth that was once in her mouth: it filled me with secret glee. Our tongues were a single territory.

Cecilia's shoulder jolted against mine, and I shivered with the memory of soggy gruel glued to the roof of my mouth. She shifted away, leaning as far from me as possible. Her disgust was enough to feed me forever.

The bus shuddered back into the leftmost lane of the highway, the dividing meridian unfurling beside us. The left side of the sky was punctured, its blood set loose as a flock of red balloons. They drifted away in the dark, a few snagging on distant trees, staticky. Cecilia and I used to rub balloons against our scalps to make our hair stand up. Her strands achieved more verticality, and mine swiveled into a halo. Afterward, I found a few hairs clinging to the globe of the balloon, and I swallowed the ones I thought were hers. To be safe, I swallowed them all.

Up at the front of the bus, the bus driver leaned forward, his head bobbing against a ceiling of cobwebs. The wigged woman stumbled back into her seat, her legs jutting into the aisle. From the back of the bus, where we were alone, I heard the woman spitting: *You're crazy! Crazy! Trying to kill us!* I watched Cecilia's reflection lean back, pressing into her plastic seat. Now that we were sitting directly beside each other, our kneecaps were neighboring mushrooms, mothered from the same dirt. She was facing ahead, smiling.

Another voice, a man's, traveling all the way to the back of the bus: *Something ran into the road.* A red plastic bag of oranges had spilled into the aisle, each wearing a bruise of a different blue, like the time-lapse of a wound. No one claimed them, and one rolled down the aisle toward my feet. I bent to pick it up, its navel leaking a thick syrup, scabbing sweet over my knuckles. Inside the rind was Cecilia, silent as a seed, watching me.

The man's voice continued to come between us: *There's no one out there. Who would be out there in the middle of the freeway?*

A deer?

There aren't any deer this far from the hills.

One time I saw a deer inside Costco.

It must have been a pigeon. They get trapped inside and die in there.

It was a deer. It was this big! This big!

The woman in the wig gestured wide, her forearms swinging like lanterns. Her hand lashed out across the aisle, smacking the shoulder of a short-haired woman who'd been asleep and was now awake. Her purse's mouth had been torn open by the sudden movement of the bus, and coins spilled into the empty seat beside her.

Beside me, Cecilia laughed. The landscape outside filled with her sound. This freeway was the only place where you could see the stars, but tonight there was only the empty sky, tender as the expanse of an eye.

Ahead of us, the passengers settled into stillness, but Cecilia lolled her head back. She was still laughing.

Because she made me afraid, because this fear fertilized my worst fantasies, I turned around in my seat and gazed out the back window of the bus, out toward the freeway.

The lane lines had faded to nothing, so the freeway was one glowing pane. I imagined how it might reflect her face if she stood on its surface, and that was when I saw it: the deer our bus had swerved to avoid. Except it didn't look like a deer. It was a woman on her hands and knees, scurrying sideways across the width of the freeway. She lowered her head as she scuttled, her belly brushing the ground, skimming the asphalt the way a dog's genitals graze the grass, pissing on what it loves. In the middle of the street, she raised her head. Except for the headlight of her mouth, her face was blank. Her skin was the color of a nickel, and there was no hair on her anywhere. Her scalp was sewn directly into the sky.

Though we must have been going at least sixty miles per hour, the woman did not recede: she stayed the same size in the back window, as if painted on the inside of the pane, then lowered her head again and continued to crawl across the street at an aphid's pace. She disappeared where the cinder-block walls stood tall.

I stared at the back window, wondering who had replaced it with a TV screen. Was this some new feature of the bus? But when the woman was gone from the windowpane, the night switched on again normally. I pressed my palms to the glass, searching for leaks in the screen, cracks in the scene. But nothing was projected onto the pane except my own face now. Cecilia turned her head to watch me kneeling on the seat, scouring the window for the source of its imagery, fingering it for a channel button.

Deer don't see red or green very well, Cecilia said. She rubbed the side of her neck, and I wondered which ache was occupying her now.

I stared at her, still kneeling, my hands roaming the window.

The bus is green, Cecilia said. *I wonder if it could see us. The deer, I mean.* I told her I'd never noticed, not once in all my life, that the bus was green.

Cecilia laughed. Then she winced and kneaded the side of her neck.

I thought the bus was bus colored, I said. *I don't think I've ever considered it any other color.*

In my mind, Cecilia was the one narrowing the night around us, cinching the sky. She was capable of manufacturing both privacy and publicity. She was inside and outside this bus simultaneously, and she refused to reveal the seams of the world she slipped between.

You keep staring at me, Cecilia said. *In the window too.*

I sat back down, facing the front of the bus again, trying to imagine what shade of green it was, if it was beer-bottle green or rusted-penny green or vein green.

Apologizing, I told her I only stared because I was concerned about her neck pain, which must have been aggravated by the bus. Cecilia shook her head slowly and said actually, when the bus swerved, she'd floated for a second in her seat. The chiropractor recommended moving in water, seeking spaces to be weightless. It was better for the spine, less pressure on the space between vertebrae.

In her presence, I didn't want to float; I preferred the humility of being dragged along on a tether.

Do you know why tigers are orange? Cecilia asked, looking down at her slack hands. There was a knob at the back of her neck, slick and twisting under the skin. *Because their prey see orange how we see green. Tigers are bright to us, but to what they hunt, they're blades of grass.*

We were both daughters born in the year of the tiger, which, according to our mothers, meant we were badly packaged. Cecilia's mother heard from a fellow hair-dresser that in her village, there was a daughter born in the year of the tiger who married a man born in the year of the rabbit. The day of their wedding, the groom's father died of TV static trapped in his heart: it electrified his whole body, turned his veins into live wiring. The wedding was waterlogged with grief, rain reproaching everyone present. Cecilia's mother didn't conclude the story, so Cecilia and I each gave it an ending: I said the daughter was sad for the groom and wept chandelier earrings, clinking crystals to wear to the burial, and Cecilia said the daughter was relieved the wedding became a funeral. Now she didn't have to pretend to be happy.

The tiger was destined to dismember the rabbit's family. Ama would say it that way. To the rabbit, the approaching tiger is a bouquet of grass, a rippling field.

As long as the tiger stays still, the rabbit will leap onto its back, feasting on its fur. Green between its teeth. Only when the rabbit digs deep into the soil, uprooting a fleshy sprout, will it realize that it's inside a mouth.

• • •

Agong's liver is the size of two palms and glistens green like the gleam of a crow's wing, and Ma says I'm not allowed to touch it until it's fully pickled. She jars it in vinegar and sets it on the windowsill, where it is mistaken for fruit and frequently swarmed by flies and bats in the evenings. The liver was not cremated with the rest of Agong's body: he had regurgitated it six months earlier and wrapped it in six pages of newspaper and bagged it in plastic and shipped it internationally to Ma's door. When she called him about the liver, he said it was my inheritance, that when I'm full grown, it will be my job to swallow it. The liver has been carried from body to body for many generations, though sometimes it skips a generation. For example, it skipped to me, and you say I'm lucky. You say you didn't get a liver from anybody, you had to just use the one you were born with. The liver in the jar is the kind that never rots or scars, not even from a lifetime of drinking or smoking or living next to a factory—Agong proved that. It wards off evil, but it is not immortal. One day it will split open in one of our bodies and hatch a crow that flees us forever, but until that day, we incubate it.

I sprinkle it with salt so it won't ripen before I'm old enough to swallow it.

Other properties of the liver are only mythical, like how it can filter blood into clean drinking water, or turn invisible if you're cut open by an organ-harvesting gang, or escape if you try to exchange it, which Agong's own aunt tried to do. Carriers of the liver often become terrified that someone will steal it in their sleep. Ma says it's never good to own anything precious. One night, Agong opened his abdomen and yanked the liver out, but the moment he tried to hand it to someone else for safekeeping, it dissolved into a flock of crows, returning years later. *Be grateful it's a liver,* Agong said, *because unlike everything else we tried to bring to you, it doesn't fray or decay, it won't be stolen or sold or pawned off. It belongs to me like a name.*

For years I pretend the liver is some kind of pet, since Ma doesn't allow pets unless they're caged and shit on a sheet—having worked so many years in shit-related industries, she refuses to touch poop voluntarily—and so I season the water with Saltine cracker crumbs and tap the side of the jar and speak all my dreams to it, especially the ones of slugs, of you. The liver never reacts, just floats at the top like the dead fish you spit. It's the purple of my thumb when I've bitten it. I never know when I am supposed to swallow it, and I suspect Ma is secretly jealous it's mine and not hers. Ama says we can have his liver and eat it too, at least the man is useful for something, that man who decided to move us here, he deserves to be pickled in his own bile, but Ma has a secret name for it and would prefer to treasure it in this jar forever, where it has no blood to barter with.

One night I'm fifteen and no longer know you. Ma is working the night shift, so I steal into the kitchen and bash it open on the floor. The liver swims in vinegar, drifting across the tiles like an island, and I wonder how it attached to Agong, if there's some kind of string that was snipped loose, or if it bounced buoyantly inside him. Agong used to tell me that islands were held in place by giants who stood underneath them, on the sea floor, and I believed this until Ama said, *Shit, shit, shit, no man can hold up an entire world.* She says if this were true, Agong's decision to move us all here would have made us rich. She says, *The problem is, poor people making money is like a tortoise crawling up a wall, and rich people making money is like a tidal wave mauling a mountain.* She says, *The problem is, you marry a chicken, you follow a chicken. You marry a dog, you follow a dog. It means you have no choice. Loyalty is your leash. You have to follow the man no matter his species. We had to follow him everywhere. You see, there are men in this world who sit on their asses until they flatten into rafts, and all we can do is ride.*

The liver nudges my knees the way dolphins on TV greet friendly strangers. I pet its back, its purple blubber, and it's silkier than I imagined, hot as a fevered forehead. I scoop it up in both hands, kissing it without tongue, and it pulses sour against my lips, blood lunging through it. When it slides down my throat, I feel myself heavy, so heavy I know I will never again be lifted by anything, and I understand something about Agong, finally, about how he obeyed only the gravity of his own liver, ignoring the pull of all other planets, needs, or pleas. If only I'd swallowed the liver sooner and regurgitated half of it into your throat, ushering you into its orbit, leasing you some of its loyalty.

• • •

Middle school is full of girls with too many syllables. Melody has a whistle-thin neck and carpools to school with the other three-syllable girls, like Tiffany and Vivian and Jennifers I, II, and III. You are a four-syllable girl whose vowels are coveted by all, and the three-syllable girls flock to feed on the *a* at the end of your name. You say you will give your fourth syllable to me, break it off like bread, and then we will each have three. I am so happy.

We hunt the crows that constellate the blacktop, running directly at them, but unlike pigeons, who are definitely prey animals, along with deer and sardines, they don't scatter into the sky. We stand shoulder to shoulder and cast our tentacled shadow into the sea of them, but the crows aren't scared of our togetherness.

Scattering the girls is a different game, and I play it alone. I dream of sprinkling their teeth on the blacktop, their spines cracking into consonants. They dip their fingers in the sweat you leave on the bench at lunch, pecking at any shine you leave behind. They beg for a little of your fourth syllable, just a mouthful, and I chase them away.

So that they will no longer hunt you, so that their spines go flaccid with fear, I plant protection: tanbark shrapnel in Melody's hot dog at lunch. When she swallows, it tears a hole in her stomach like a toe through a sock. She has to be resurrected at the Taiwanese Buddhist temple, where Ma tells me to pay back my karmic debt and become a nun. I shave my head and commit myself to nunhood for six months, eating only plain tofu, unsalted broth, and diced boiled taro. (Except Ma says I would look ugly bald and no one will want to marry me, so she tells me to wear a swim cap instead of actually shaving my head. Though neither of us can swim, you say you prefer me with the cap on, that now I look like a plucked chicken.) As a junior nun, I have to spend weekends dumping buckets of burned names. In the parking lot, we incinerate the names of everyone who has been dead a hundred days. The buckets froth with ash and retired light, and sometimes when I stir a chopstick around in it, I roll over a molar. The nuns claim not to be burning any bodies, only names written on white paper, but one time I empty a bucket and there's a shin in it. Bent like a boomerang and with some fat still swathing it.

Melody comes in with her mother a few times during the morning service. I avert my eyes and hide inside the brass bell for the full four hours. Afterward, I see Melody in the parking lot, kneeling in front of a bucket, burning her own name, the smoke obscuring her face. Ma says that because of me, Melody has a plastic bag in her belly, lining her like a trash can. You are impressed by this and say that I did her a favor by killing her, because a double-lined belly is way safer, just think of the things you could do without worry, such as sword-swallowing or partial impalement. She is 100 percent leakproof. At the temple, the nuns show me VHS tapes of enlightenment, how you can be knocked from your body like a loose tooth and live rootless. They show me recordings of nuns sitting on flaming coals, rolling through meadows of needles, dragging pickup trucks through the mud with their teeth, meditating for weeks in subzero temperatures. It's all possible, they say, if you detach from desire. I think of your kneecaps and shriek. I think of your sweat and how it was sweet for a week instead of salty, and you told me you were just reversing your body for a while, that your eyes were now pointed toward the back of your head, seeing inside your skull, and that your knees hinged the other way. You stand below me while I dangle upside down from the monkey bars, disappointed that my knees only hook one way, and you say, *Don't worry, I'm the sea and will swallow you if you fall.* Never have I been so grateful to be small, to float in your palm.

At the temple, I search the parking lot for the bucket Melody was burned in. I pour the ashes onto my bare feet and remember what the nuns said, that desire is detachable as a doll limb. *Discard it,* they said, and I grill my feet into shrimp, tender and lemoned. Next time Melody comes, I think I'll toothpick my toes and feed them to her. She'll refuse and say I killed her, unstringing the beads of her name and spitting them at me. Her hatred will be a comfort to me, a stone I'll turn and turn under my tongue.

I prefer it when you like boys, because that's no threat at all. Liking a boy is the same as liking a dog or a fish. There is a limit to what you can share with it, since your tongues are different sizes. When I witness the boys talking to you, it's like watching someone reel a shoelace into the endless sea, expecting to fish out something. Their language is only so long, and it cannot reach you. But I reach you lower down than any of them, I reach you lower down than love.

At the tinny lunch table outside, you say you've noticed I've been copying the way you eat. For the first time, I am made aware of my shame: in my family, shame doesn't need to be seen. It's air, everywhere. It's a condition of living, as inborn as a hip bone, the hilt by which you hold everything. Shame is our skin, and all the living and the dead touch us through it. Life can't lean directly on our meat. Shame can even predate you: when Ma was little, she was ashamed that none of her older sisters were sons, that she was the sixth and last chance for the family to have a son, that her children would someday truncate the surname. Structurally, a daughter cannot belong to her family. She can only be discarded by it.

You notice the way I bite open the casing at the end of the hot dog before sucking out its meat, which is smooth as sofa foam. You say I am copying the way you eat. In my shame, I turn my eyes away, afraid you will know I'm empty. That I copy you to be occupied by you.

You look down at our hot dogs cradled in their cardboard cartons and ask me to eat. *Do it now,* you say, so I pick up my hot dog, leaving its bun bereft. But I don't know how to eat it without watching you first, don't know how to prove that my mouth functions on its own. So I fasten my teeth like flies to the knotted casing, begin nibbling, praying that from your angle, I don't resemble anything. *Aha, I caught you,* you say, jutting your finger into my cheek. You twist the hot dog out of my fist and lick it from end to end, lathing it with your tongue, dropping it back into its soggy bed. This, you are convinced, has ruined it. The other girls watch us and laugh, but I recognize the hunger in their eyes: like the crows, they are waiting to swoop in and steal you from me. Though I pretend to say a final good-bye, carrying the tray to the trash can rimmed with crows, I ensure that the hot dog slides onto the surface of the garbage. For the rest of lunch, while you skin your hot dog with your teeth, I sit beside you and fend off the crows from afar, guarding the can with my eyes, warning them away. For once, they obey me and flee. They are creatures of the future, and they remember all the ways I'll hurt them someday.

You're a crow mouth, you say, *Wu ya zui.* I stare at your mouth. You wear mustard and ketchup as lipstick, so committed to being delicious. I look down at the blacktop. A beak grows out of my shadow, a black scythe swinging for your head. I shudder and touch my lips, reassured by their tenderness. *You're lying,* I say, but my shadow is deeper than me. I'm only skin and meat, but my shadow is a sea. If I stand up, I'll slip inside it and never surface. Pinching the hot dog, you shake your head and laugh. *It's not like that. It means whatever you say will come true. But only the bad things.* Ama once told me that crows are bad luck. I turn away from my shadow and watch your hands instead, your fingers pecking the ends of the hot dog. *What bad things?* I ask. *What have I said?* Your eyes migrate into the sky, and I'm afraid you'll fly away too. *Never mind,* you say. *If you have to ask, it means you can't make anything happen.* My mouth is vacant. It can't even fill its own shadow. The only thing I can predict is emptiness.

(If only the bad things come true, here is what I pray in private: Cecilia will never escape me. Not even when we come back for our next lives. If she is a sky, I'll be light. If she's a mutt, I'll be her musk. It's okay if I don't have a body. That way she won't be burdened by me.)

At the end of lunch, when it's time to be herded back into the classroom, I linger behind and pretend to throw something in the trash when really I'm darting my hand into the can, fishing out the hot dog. The crows know I'm one of them, dedicated to the discarded. Desperate to fill myself.

In the bathroom at recess, the three-syllable girls gather to practice kissing, marrying their openings. We slide under the stall door to join them, and the girls repeat the rules: When you kiss, there has to be a witness. You have to be in a group of at least three. One of you is the man, the other is the woman, and the other is the baby inside the woman. If you're the baby, you have to be quiet and shut your eyes like you're inside a belly. If you open them to watch, you can't say a word, you can only suck your thumb and cry when you've shit yourself.

There are three girls in the stall with us, Melody who I killed once, Vivian who wears a bell around her wrist so her mother can always hear her, and Jennifer II who used to eat ants. Melody is the woman, so she braids her arms around Jennifer II's neck, and Jennifer II is the man, so she puts her hands around Melody's waist. Vivian is the baby, so she squats on the toilet and suckles at her pinky, pretending to watch from inside another body.

We stand with our backs against the stall door, its green paint flaking off on our shoulders, watching Melody marry Jennifer II. Melody's tongue thrashes like it's drowning, and Jennifer II tries not to bite down on it. I pretend we're watching the three-syllable girls through a screen, that there is a pane of crystallized light between us and this marriage. Even in the square of this stall, even when our breath knits into fog and rises off the tiles, I have to imagine that the two of us are separate from them.

I feed on our solitude: after school, whenever our mothers can't pick us up, the teacher lets us play on the computer in the library, the one shaped like an astronaut's helmet. We play a wedding game on the monitor. The girl begins naked, wearing a white bra and panties, and we drag wedding dresses on top of her, fitting her bald head with hair, sketching shadows onto her eyelids with our cursors. When we finish deciding on the length of the gown—I like the knees exposed, but you say only horses get married in short dresses—a window pops up and asks whether we want to print the body. But we aren't allowed to use the library printer, so we print the bride in our minds. To do this, we have to stare as hard as we can at the screen, then shut our eyes and recite the important details. Sweetheart neckline. Hemline sweeping the floor. Veil clinging to her shoulders like condensation on a window. *When we grow up,* you say—it is the first time I hear you address the future directly—*we'll need to access this file of brides, so we should store it on the shallowest shelf of our minds, somewhere we can reach easily.* You ask me where I want to get married (you say beach, I say church, though we've been to neither), how many bridesmaids (you say a hundred and I say none), what kind of flowers (you say Venus flytraps, because flies can ruin public gatherings, and I say lilies of the valley), but we always forget to imagine the groom, and so the men in my mind remain faceless, blank and bald as melons, like the girls on screen before we choose the color and size of their eyes (green nickels).

I imagine Melody and Jennifer II as those girls we gown, our cursors pulling on their clothes, hacking off their limbs, shaving their scalps, dashing strands of their hair upon the green bathroom tiles. The stall door is cold against my back, cold as a glass screen, and I replace

Jennifer II's face with yours. On screen, it's easy as swiping her mouth to the side, dragging in a new pair of salt-shriveled lips to replace them, hovering my cursor under her left eye to mark your mole. Melody, I yank off screen by the hair, dissolving her flaccid tongue in the blue acid of a sea-themed screensaver. Into her place, I drag myself, husked of my hair and face, a blank template. Between my legs, I position a slug, something she loves.

Melody and Jennifer II unlatch mouths. Their separation is squelching. Crows batter the stall door, bruising me between the shoulder blades. You and I have not touched, have only watched. Jennifer turns toward us and says, *Because I'm the man, I let her go.*

Do you want to try now? she asks us. She says she can pretend to be the baby, she can even curl and touch her forehead to her belly button, look. Beside me, I hear the sharp bones of your shoulders scrape up and down the stall door. You shrug and say you don't know, you've never done it before. *It's practice,* Melody says, and explains that at night, she twists her blanket into a wick and tucks it between her legs—sometimes she uses her jump rope—and when it lights up beneath her, she imagines a baby filling her belly. *You have to imagine it daily,* she explains, *or else one day when you really do have a baby, your belly will have gone its whole life never expecting to get that big, and it'll explode. Imagining is practicing,* she says, but you just keep shrugging.

Against the stall, the crows beat their wings bald. I don't dare to look at you, afraid you might see what wades in my eyes. If Melody is right, if there is no difference between doing something and dreaming it, it means I have violated you many times. In my dreams, you stand before me in this bathroom, the mirrors flanking you like wings. In their reflection, I stand faceless and bald, ready to be made. Because I'm afraid of exiting before the computer has finished saving, I don't blink, don't risk shutting my eyelids. Unlike mine, your face remains, all your features self-arranged and unable to be replaced, not even when I reach out to flick the mole beneath your eye, trying to shoo it away like a fly. I don't want a witness for this part, when I pry open your jaws, when I plunge my fingers into the soil of your throat and scour for what you've swallowed. What seed did you sprout from, springing up whole and self-sustained? How did you come to possess yourself? My forefinger is caught in a chokehold, and when I shimmy it out of your throat, I find a soda-can tab ringing my knuckle. It looks like a hollowed nickel. This isn't it, I think, this can't be it. How can it be true, that something this small is the reason I love you? I refuse to believe it. If it's true, if you and I are equally empty, harboring only the tiniest of souls, then why are you the direction of my longing? Why do I turn away from myself? Once again, I yank your mouth open, and though your teeth snap and your pores distort in pain, I do not stop. Your protests patter my skin, your cries slide off me like the rain.

After the day of our practice marriage, when our ceremony was soiled by the presence of others, I begin to have trouble looking into the bathroom mirrors. I avoid peeing at school entirely. Unable to enter the bathroom, I find myself standing at the threshold, believing that if I inhale the perfume of other people's urine, it will somehow fulfill my body's urge to produce its own.

When I look at mirrors, even the side mirrors of buses, even puddles in the gutter, too dull to distinguish a face from a flock of crows, I have to open my mouth. It's an automated muscle, a terrifying tic. I gape until my jaw radiates pain, punishing me for the dream of prying you open. Suctioned to the mirror's scarred silver, I look out through the pinhole of my throat. Wondering what you left inside me, after all these years, that I still can't say.

• • •

In middle school, the other kids get picked up at the circular curb, scuttling like cockroaches into minivans and station wagons, but we stay late. Our mothers are working nights and lag behind the light. We are supposed to take the bus, but you miss it on purpose so we can play on the computer in the library. That's how you phrase it: play. The windows of the library are dim as sleeping screens, and I only know they're alive because they flinch a little when tree branches fork into their sides. The other kids call them tampon trees: in the summer, they swell with little white flowers that smell like menstrual blood. On the computer, you find their name: ornamental pear trees, native to Asia. They grow easily in a variety of climates, you read aloud, then laugh and say the whole school smells like a crotch. Then you ask if I want to look at porn. The library is empty, the light of the screen drilling into me.

The video plays on mute. *He's peeing into her mouth,* I whisper, and you shake your head. *It's not pee,* you say, *it just comes out of the same hole.* But if it comes out of the same hole, how do you know if it's pee or not?

Instead of answering, you say, *Shut up, she knows.* You watch the screen and I watch your face, light hissing into vapor where it touches your cheek. The more I stare at you, the more my shadow loses touch with the floor, the more I disappear. I rub my feet on the carpet, then glance again at the screen. The librarian lumbers out from behind a shelf, and you click pause, drag out the window of our wedding dresses. When she disappears again, I tell you I want to watch two men. It's easier for me to be aroused by our absence. To erase ourselves as subjects. The cries of the women ring false to me, maybe because it's not a fantasy to be in pain; it's too easily achievable. Routine. I pray for a pleasure that reaches me from the future, a want that is infinitely beyond, a horizon that refuses to be hounded. I want to be near you in a state of ecstatic exile.

You say it's disgusting to watch men, you'd rather watch two women, so I say nothing. You reopen the window. I can hear your breath curl in your mouth like an animal. Your hands harass the elastic waistband of your pants. In class, boys call our names, so we turn around.

They form a hole with their thumb and forefinger, then insert their other forefinger into the hole, sawing it in and out, waiting for us to react. I look away, but you laugh as loud as you can. As if the sound can shield us. As if a finger feels nothing.

Sitting in the dim light, I watch you blink, your eyelashes lapping up the space between us and the screen. The tips of your lashes moisten with tears, and I want a tongue small enough to lick each one clean. Your neck throbs, skin stretched taut around your pulse like the head of a drum. I am struck by your blood. You hoist your hand into my lap, one thumb beneath my shirt, the tip of it filling my belly button, burrowing until I bleed.

Flicking the thin skin that lids my belly button, your thumb nudges like a worm toward dirt, delighting in the dark. Your path through me is the same as decay's, and my flesh parts from the stone pit of my stomach, exposing a hollow that swallows.

When I mouth for mercy, the chair squeals, and the librarian pokes her head in our direction. We stand up to leave, my shirt welded to my belly button, the ditch of skin welling with blood and pus. I pull at the fabric, peel open the sore like a sweet. I look inside it. The hole darkens and fills with your pupil.

• • •

We were reaching the end of the line. Sweat surged down my spine, and I wanted to fling myself out the back windshield of the bus. The faceless woman still scurried behind us, chugging from the exhaust pipe, mouthing for a nipple, wordless and wanting. But this must be an illusion: if she were faceless, she couldn't be watching or trying to latch to the bus, and the gaze I felt must belong to someone else. Something cold wept down the crook of my arm, and I shivered in my hard seat.

Cecilia shifted away from me, straddling two seats. Unwilling to commit to a single space. Outside the windows were the bleached streaks of empty trains, asleep in their chain-link yards, rows of them like teeth. When I was little, I didn't understand that trains also took breaks, and I thought Ma was just driving so fast that it made the trains beside the freeway look like they were still.

We passed the trains, and I twisted around to look back at them. They were amorphous now, sloppy as slugs, their metallic shells dissolving to reveal yolk-soft bodies. There were billboards staked along the freeway, and I swore they were just the same one repeating over and over: either the bus was sliding in place, reiterating the same piece of street, or a single person had purchased these billboards for miles, and I couldn't decide which was more horrifying. On each billboard was an ad for an exterminator, and though I couldn't read the details, I recognized the exterminator's face. It was plastered on the handles of shopping carts and pasted to telephone poles and often dolloped with crowshit. Every time her face flapped by on a billboard, it looked different, distorted, and I didn't know if it was because we were moving so fast or if her face was actually changing, each billboard aging at its own pace. In one, she was wearing a full beard, and in another, her mouth jutted out like an udder.

The woman, if I remembered right, killed raccoons for a living. Though she didn't advertise killing, only the vague process of removal. Another one of her faces flicked past, and this time, her cheeks were greasy-furred, her eyes ringed like a raccoon's. I turned to Cecilia to ask if she, too, had noticed that all the billboards contained the same face, and I was surprised to see she was looking at me.

Because I needed some way to divert her, I scrabbled at the surface of my mind for something to say: *Raccoons are predators,* I said. *Or are they scavengers? Is there a difference between seeking live meat and dead meat?* Like crows, the local raccoons were attracted to trash, and because of this, they were sometimes electrified or shot with air rifles or removed by professionals. I wondered if, like the crows, they loathed certain colors of light, repelled by the shine of green eyes. There was once a raccoon that nested in the insulation of our duplex, burrowing into the plaster between our unit and the neighbor's. The walls became porous and phlegmy, pores puckering everywhere I touched. A pink tongue flicked out of an electrical outlet's slit, licking my ankle as I walked past, though Ma said I'd imagined it. She said she wasn't going to tell the landlord about the raccoon: it was spring, she explained, and the raccoon was there to give birth. It would leave with the season. Inside the walls, I wondered how many babies it had, how they were all able to breathe, but when I pressed my ear up to the plaster, I could only hear scratching and stirring, nails scaling. At night, when the sound was loudest, I wondered what would happen if the raccoon or its babies died, how we would know if they'd left or been suffocated, how we would carve the bodies out, if the landlord would fine us, whether raccoons preferred cremation or burial, whose job it was to mourn the death of predators, if you had to mourn all the fertile quail eggs they stole and the doves they plucked, if alongside their own lives, you had to grieve all the ones they'd swallowed.

Cecilia didn't answer me. I wondered if maybe I hadn't spoken my question aloud. It occurred to me that I'd barely said anything out loud this entire bus ride. But then Cecilia opened her mouth, sighed.

I didn't remember ever hearing her sigh before. Her breath lingered in the air, a thick mist mustering heat, fogging the windows.

The bus must have resembled a quill, a shaft once filled with blood. We drifted toward an exit, no longer on the freeway, and in this new city, there were no streetlights. Our headlights plunged into the night and met the resistance of a muscled dark.

I didn't recognize this dark, and the electronic ticker tape at the front of the bus flashed the name of a stop I didn't know: the letters were scrambled. The light of that illegible name slid across Cecilia's face like a tongue.

Do you know where we are? I asked her. The street seemed to warp as we drove over it, unstapled from a surface. Every time we stopped, the blacktop bucked beneath us. Even the stoplights here didn't look like the swinging pendants that hung from the neck of the city we'd left; they resembled dangling crow carcasses, their eyes alternating green, green, green. There must have been houses and apartments and sidewalks beside us, but darkness sloshed across the windows, obscuring everything.

A little, Cecilia said. The space between my question and her answer felt unbearably stretched, and if she'd been silent for just a moment longer, something would have snapped between us. I would have said I was angry at her for appearing again in the screens of these windows, my life. I was angry I couldn't touch her, that my memories of her were entombed in meat and muscle and gristle, monumental. Move out of the way, I wanted to say, so I can see you better.

Cecilia laughed, and as if she'd heard me, she said, *You keep disappearing. You haven't really said a word to me.*

The more I see you, I said, turning to the window, *the more you mean nothing to me. I wish you would leave.* I didn't know if this was a city or my own mind. The landscapes were the same. The bus was suddenly empty, though I didn't remember ever stopping. We must have stopped, and passengers must have slid off their saddles. Must have dismounted from their desires.

Cecilia shifted in her seat, the sleeves of her jacket deflating. It made her look birdlike, the way she could suddenly flatten herself, retract her heat to her skin.

I'm practicing, she said. She turned to face the opposite window, the one on her left. *Come with me.*

Why did you wait for me at the bus stop? Why didn't you just leave? I asked. In a way, I'd never waited for her, or maybe I'd only ever waited for her absence. I shelled my memories and fled with them, the way a rodent will find some jewel of a seed and flee to feast on it alone, avoiding potential theft, minimizing loss. It was possible that from the beginning, I was plucking her apart, twisting loose her organs like fruit, tucking them into my maw, ready to flee and eat in peace. Maybe my fantasy was not our aloneness. Maybe I only wanted to be alone with desire, and to do that, I had to destroy her. The braid of my brain came apart in my hands. I didn't want to know anything about her life, what she did to live, where she slept, how many times a day she wiped her ass, the last time she cut her hair, whether she confused the words *fray* and *flay*. All those details would obscure her. All those details would uproot what I knew of her, and I couldn't bear her as a stranger. Her presence was limited by skin, bounded by it. But her absence could touch me anywhere, everywhere. It was pure. In my mind I repeated: *Disappear now, so I can keep what I keep. Please.*

It would be better now if you were dead, I might've said. Whether I said it or not, she responded: *If I died, do you really think I'd be leaving? When has death ever meant left?*

At home, crows hid their nuts beneath our roof tiles, futures to go back to. I heard a heavier animal running across the roof at night, broken tiles sprinkling down.

Maybe my sleep was turning dense as sleet, thudding the roof with its hooves. The mystery of that animal was comforting, an unhealed hole in me, an absence I cooed to.

Above us, hundreds of slugs splattered the roof of the bus.

• • •

The TV is always on, spitting light into our skulls. When other faces flicker across theirs, Ma and Ama are striped into another species, their teeth off leash, and I'm relieved that they look like me, predatory. When the TV is off, their faces return to being human, and I miss their former cruelty.

On the shopping channel, Ama's favorite, I overhear a commercial for a cream that erases crow's-feet, which are something you grow when you're old. I glance at Ama beside me, a blanket surrounding her like a lake, her legs tucked into its depths, and I imagine that underneath, she has sprouted the feet of a crow, scaly and taloned. I look at her sideways, trying to guess the next limb that will diverge into a bird. Someday, when Ama is a crow, I won't be alone: she'll be just like me, a body in between.

Our TV was fished from a dumpster long ago, and its screen is webbed with cracks. They glow like the veins in an egg's membrane. I wonder if that's why the lovebird lives on top of the TV, if it believes it is incubating an egg, mistaking the shadows on screen for the squirm of birth. I cover its cage with a towel. I don't want it to know the egg is infertile. Ma and Ama watch the screen between shifts, and I fall asleep every night to the sound of its light clawing up our walls. Ma says that babies recognize the voices they heard in the womb. That sound is what I'm braised in. She says I suckled on the TV screen when I was a baby, trying to nurse from it. Mistaking lines of subtitles for ribbons of milk.

When I sprawl across their laps on the sofa, Ma and Ama watch a TV show about a man who strands himself in extreme environments and tries to survive alone. Once, he spent a week on a boat in the middle of the Pacific, weaving his beard hairs into an oar, and another time, he was dropped in the center of a jungle we come from. I gnaw my fist while I watch, but Ama always reminds me it's staged, there's no real risk: he can't really be alone when there's a whole crew filming, helicopters collecting footage from above, ready at any time to descend.

At school, I tell you the TV man voluntarily lived in the desert for ten nights and drank his own pee. The desert is quilled with man-high cacti that shine in the dark, tapered like crow's feathers, and inside their spines is usually water, except this year there's a drought and the cacti are hollow jawbones and the desert has dry mouth. Is it possible for a desert to experience drought? Isn't that like the sea experiencing wetness? But you don't answer me. You become fixated on this single episode, and on the playground, three minutes into recess, you say it's time for us to drink our own pee, given that no one has found us yet, and no one is even looking. You dare me to drink first, but neither of us brought a receptacle to capture the pee, so I have to become your live faucet. You crouch in front of me while I pull down my brother's hand-me-down jersey shorts, their hems detaching into peninsulas. *Aim for my mouth,* you say. *So we don't waste any water and I won't have to die out here alone.* We cluster together behind a birch tree splintering out of the ground like a compound fracture. With my back against the bark, I widen my legs and try my best to aim, visualizing the trajectory and squatting over your face, my shadow tenting you, my hands held out like guardrails, but I still end up spraying mostly your shirt and shoulders and, mysteriously, both elbows. The most accurate droplet bedazzles your chin and bursts open before you can lick it or wipe it away. I have failed to keep you alive. When you go to the lost and found to change clothes before class, explaining that you've wet yourself, the lady in the office asks if you've somehow managed to pee upside down. But you reveal nothing.

You say we can't tell anyone we've been stranded in the desert. I agree; I know that unlike in the TV show, there's no one documenting us. There's no one to helicopter us in or out. Our thirst isn't turned into plot. But as long as we keep it a secret, as long as our desert spans only the two of our bodies, no one can contradict us. No one can say we aren't skeletons already, bones pummeled by hot wind, pulverized into sand.

This is the summer we hear that Cecilia, the real one, got caught up in a sex scandal that Ma and the neighbors talk about every evening. Apparently, some actor made movies of himself having sex with all these actresses, and the footage has been made public. Ma is the one who found the video and forwarded the link to all the neighbors, who sent us thank-you notes and free green bananas for weeks. On the phone, I listen while Ma talks about it with my aunts, but all I overhear is that they've seen her pubic hair, and that there's a lot of it. *She's got a full bush down there! I laughed my belly broken! I laugh through a hole in my stomach now! I mean, a woman as rich as that, you'd expect her to know how to shave,* Ma says. *Someone should get her a Weedwacker. The one that's As Seen on TV. We've all seen her on TV!* For a moment I feel a sprinkling of superiority, since you are hairier than me, but this feeling dissipates as soon as Ma hangs up.

Well, Ma says to me, *you've got nothing down there anyway, so you wouldn't know what it means to get rid of anything.* Then she talks with my ama for another hour about angles, cloudy lighting, how she saw one of Cecilia's movies on TV recently, the one where she plays the love interest of a cop who's undercover in a drug ring, how a car explodes as soon as she tumbles out of it, how it was impossible to see her face, jeweled in fake blood, without seeing the cameraman's shadow crossing over it.

After so much time delaying my arrival to your apartment, you tell me finally that even though there's no AC, your mother just bought new electric fans at the dollar store, and now it's cooler for us to cocoon up there. I'm so excited about seeing where you sleep and dream and drool that I forget to go to the bathroom for hours before coming over, and when I run up the three flights of stairs to your door, I have to take small steps so my legs don't scissor open and enable the spray. Your door is the one plastered with a Post-it note sheared into the shape of a koi. *To welcome wealth into the home,* you say. According to my ma, money is like a man, it never stays, it always disappoints you. You told me once that your father was dead. Mine too, I said, though I wasn't sure that was true. I wanted you to think my father was dead so we could co-own something, or at least you could loan me your loss. I could wear your grief secondhand, like my older cousins' shirts, which were shipped to me every year and smelled of the men who undressed them.

We sit cross legged on a sheet of newspaper spread in your living room. According to you, the newspaper protects the hardwood floor beneath, especially because sweat from the soles of the feet can degrade wood. I don't tell you that sounds stupid, like when my neighbor tells me not to stand next to microwaves because the radiation might stop my menstrual cycle. In your presence, belief is mandatory.

You say you have the TV ready to show me your mother singing, another thing I'm willing to believe. Her lungs will be laced with lyrics, her mouth wrapped around the apple of a microphone, but the TV won't turn on. Its screen liquefies in the heat, puddling between our feet. It's balanced on a stack of newspapers, and I sus-pect it's always been broken, that you've been lying from the beginning, just like Ma said. When I told Ma what you'd said about your mother, she laughed and said, *That woman? That woman is pretty much nameless. She's about as well known as an eighteenth-tier city. I would recognize her if she used to sing on TV. But her face means shit to me. Besides, being famous is just another form of slaughter. Haven't you heard that saying? People fear fame the way pigs fear fatten-ing. To be seen is slaughter.* But I don't say anything: your lies provide all the light in my life.

You knee the TV screen, watch it solidify into a bruise. You beat the side of the set with both fists until it hacks up static. I ask if you've heard about the scan-dal, about the real Cecilia, your namesake. Sitting back on your heels, you elbow the screen and say shut up: *You don't know anything about actresses, about performance.* According to you, the whole scandal has been acted out: *It's acting. I know acting. My mother and I watch TV every night until morning, and she points it out to me, when the actors are just fake-acting and when they're real-acting.*

Aren't those the same, I say, but you shake your head. Your two braids lasso your face. *No,* you say, *when you're a real actor, you're supposed to believe it's real life. It's so real you don't even remember your name, your mother, your birthmarks.* You tell me the real Cecilia knows that kind of acting: *So you see, that video just looks so real that every-one really believes it's her body.* In the dead TV screen's reflection, you teach me how to open my mouth the way singers do, not big like I'm swallowing flies but big like I'm trying to bury all the sky's light.

One last time, you headbutt the TV until the screen cracks into a mosaic, blue veins swelling with light. But it still won't turn on. I sweat through the newspaper you laid out for me, stewing in its ink, praying what's on the newsprint won't transfer to my ass, that I won't get slapped for dirtying my pants. I ask when your mother is coming back. Plastic fans are plugged into the wall, their helicopter blades whirling, but they still aren't able to lift off. I always thought it was sad that they worked so hard and never got off the ground. *I don't know,* you say, *she might be working all night.* I used to think working nights meant you were the moon, that somehow the night couldn't run without you, but it turns out your mother cleaned things while people were sleeping. *She does it here too,* you say. *One time I woke up and she was scouring my arms with steel wool. She told me that's how you get the hair off permanently.*

I think about the famous Cecilia and the lack of hair between my legs, glancing down at my lap, wondering when I'll grow a shadow of my own. *But you've got no hair on your arms,* I say. *That's because my mother's cleaned me,* you say, explaining that someday, you'll do the same to me, show me how to remove my fur without any blood escaping.

Sorry the TV's broken, you say, but apologies never surface fully in your mouth, instead staying submerged beneath your tongue. *It's okay,* I say, and tell you it's always on in my house anyway. For the first time, I am aware of the silence in the apartment, the quiet swelling of a kneecap, your neighbors pressed to the walls, trying to listen in on this silence, trying to siphon it for themselves.

Let's make our own TV, you say, and I think at first you want to build one, though there's nothing in the room except sofa cushions and fans and bowls of fruit and newspapers stickered to our asses, plus a full-length mirror leaning on the wall beside the television set. *No,* you say. *I mean, let's make a movie.*

What kind of movie, I say, thinking of all the Hong Kong gangster movies Ama bought from the man who spread a blanket at the bus stop. Those movies proved to me that men weren't myths, that sometimes they exploded or fell out of buildings or stabbed each other to prove the softness of their intestines.

When I tell you I like gangster movies, you say you hate those bootlegs. *They're all shaky, and you can see the shadows of people standing up to go pee. Let's make a real movie, like Cecilia,* you say, though I enjoy seeing the audience in the foreground of those DVDs, because it makes looking feel less lonely. The audience is an extension of my body. One time I heard someone fart during an explosion scene, and for a few seconds I could smell it on my side of the screen.

Then I realize you mean the other movie, the tape neither of us has seen. You stand in front of me in your denim shorts, hand-me-downs from no one, the hairbands cuffed around your wrist, your stretchy headband. I envy the way you dress, like someone in a catalog—not the main model but one of the background girls, blurry and out of focus, surrounding the scene.

I'll be Cecilia, you say, your bangs damp and plastered to your temples. *You be the man.* I think of Melody in the bathroom stall, teaching me that a man's hands go around the waist and a woman's hands go around the neck. Neither of us knows the name of the man in the tape, and Ma hasn't said much about him either—he's not as famous, Ma says, he still needs fattening.

Okay, I say, *but we don't have anything to film with.* You say, *So just pretend there's a camera here. It's called real-acting.* You lay down on the splayed newspapers, see-through with sweat, and I lean over you, straddling your hips, my brother's hand-me-down soccer shorts balling around my thighs.

What do I do, I say, and you say you don't know, try a grind. I tremble, thinking about the screens we've touched through, the directness of our current positions. I think of the meat grinder at the grocery store, the way it minces pork into pebbles, ribs into rhinestones. I rub my belly against your belly, trying to press our buttons together, to meet where our skins are thinnest. But you squirm beneath me and say, *Stop, it tickles, you aren't doing this right.* You reach up and snag my neck, then tug me down so my face is above yours, your tongue butterflying on the tip of my nose, your mouth so close I can see the blood pulsing in your molars. *Imagining is practicing,*

Melody said in the bathroom stall. But I don't know what we're practicing now, what shape we're supposed to make.

You shepherd my hips with your hands, gripping them so we're hinged together, and then you say I need to knead your chest. *Okay,* I say. *No,* you say, *I mean underneath my shirt. Okay,* I say again. Your windows are dusty and the light comes in garbled, crumbling before it reaches us. You say this is the part when the man does something. *Okay,* I say, *what.* You tell me to touch you between the legs, so I pull down your underwear and fish around in the dark with my fingers. *Not there,* you say. *That's where I go poop,* you say, *stop.* I withdraw my hand. The tips of my fingers are wet with something, and when I bring them to my lips, you say, *No, no, wait.* Too late, I taste it. Mud from the moon. A speck of it on my lower lip, wet as a sore. Strange sweet. I bend and spit, aim for the newspaper under my knees, but I miss. A green grape of my spit, its seed made of your shit. For a second I am overwhelmed by a sense of tenderness toward it, this rot foraged from both our bodies, but then I gag, an involuntary heave, and you shift and wriggle beneath me.

My fingers are sucked clean, glowing, and you snatch them out of the air, burying them in your fist. *It isn't right. It isn't right. The movie is over,* you say. *Cut, cut, cut.* You throttle my fingers and twist, but they remain stubbornly attached to my hand. At last you let go, and my hands flutter to your stomach, settling like evidence. Your body stills, your face turns away, and there is silence. It scrapes the air clean, revealing us clearly. For the first time, I realize that we are alone in our bodies, tuned into our own time. What happens inside you is happening outside of me. What happens now is ownerless.

I crawl off you, the tips of my fingers stinging, and you say I'm bad at being the man. The newspaper is wet beneath you, blank as onion peel, and now all my fingers stink as if I've been sucking on them. *My mother's gonna be home soon,* you say, but I know it isn't true. When I don't move, you speak slowly, loudly, letting each word set like a stain: *You know we shouldn't be doing this.* I stare down at the newspaper that spans the floor, expecting to see those words written in the ink bleeding across our knees. When I look up, you raise your eyebrows the way our teachers do when we stray from a line or misbehave, amused and disapproving at the same time. I flinch, recoiling like I've been hit. The truth is, I hadn't known. Hadn't even suspected we shouldn't be doing this. Suddenly, all the moments that have led to this one—asking to see your apartment, bending over the shrine of your stomach—stink up the room like a carcass. All my memories are rotting, and I scan for somewhere to discard them quickly. It would be unbearable if you caught me with them, clutching them like my precious offspring.

I nod once, twice, pretending that I, too, know all this is wrong. You nod back, confirming what I've long suspected: that everyone in this world was born with an innate knowledge of what can and cannot be touched, what deserves light and what must die in the dark, and

I alone was born without this manual, this vital organ. It was not uploaded into my body, and now my anatomy is incomplete, hardly human. While I have been a foolish animal, a slobbering dog oblivious to its owner's indulgence, you have possessed some secret restraint this whole time, indicting me in your mind while your body collaborated with mine. I cannot even feel bitter or betrayed, because I am the one who has breached normalcy, who has been hopelessly frolicking in my own feces. *We shouldn't be doing this,* you repeat, and I grip your words in my fist, make them work on me like a whip.

I remember when you said the ears, eyes, mouth, and nose are all the same tunnel. My urge is to shit on these sheets of newspaper, wipe myself clean on your eyelids, and pray that my filth is mailed to your mouth. Once, I saw a red-tailed hawk uproot a chicken from the ground. It was the neighbor's white silkie hen, pretty as a pile of snowfall. It screamed inside the hawk's mouth, its cry like a comet, suspended in the sky long after it was gone. That shriek was still a source of light in the neighborhood. The hawk didn't seem eager to shut it off, and in fact had enjoyed wrestling with the silkie in the side yard, perhaps assured by the rigor of its prey, the liveliness of its meat. Ma chased it off with a broom. *It's a juvenile,* she said. *It's only practicing. Not even eating it.* I am the same, I thought, I only practice. In the stall of the bathroom, in front of a screen, in your movie. All of it is only practice, and yet I had somehow forgotten that. I had succumbed every time we touched, while you stood back and watched from the top window of a tower, castled inside a throat of stone. Unbreachable.

Because the hawk wasn't eating its prey, just rehearsing, we found the silkie in the gravel beneath the neighbor's tree, decapitated. It continued to cry even after it was buried, and at night I knelt in the dirt and thrust my head into the soil, trying to coax its scream into my throat, trying to house that sound. If I shouted now, I thought, if my mouth mimicked yours, I would be absolved.

I watch you button your denim shorts, still repeating your words to me. Then you are silent, looking down at the done-up buttons as if they will pry themselves open again. To fill the silence, I ask if I could come back when the TV's fixed, if I could watch your mother sing then, and you nod at me. There's spit bleaching your hair. I wonder whose. I think of your mouth saying *go/no/again*, all the shapes you can sour into.

You don't say good-bye. The door hinge squeaks your name. While I walk down the stairs, I hear you behind me, humming something as you shut the door, and the whole walk home I try to remember it, the way your mouth might have said come back. *What about the movie*, I say, before you close the door fully, before your face recedes into the crack. You keep looking behind you at the sodden newspaper, at my spit on the floor with its harvested core. You look at it as if you don't recognize it, and I feel that same tenderness, the desire to scoop it up from the floor and cradle it in my mouth, until it can be loved again in the privacy of a body.

What about our footage? I ask. You shiver and say, *Don't worry, I won't release it. I won't make the same mistake she did.* I say it wasn't Cecilia who released it, the man did that, and you say, *Yes, and there's no man here, so don't worry, no one will see it.* The whole walk home I rewind it in my mind, editing your mouth into an ending, imagining a screen as wide as our skin, the way we would look on it, lit up and no one listening to us. If I'd told you that no one was watching, that any movie we starred in would be released only on the moon, would you have agreed to continue? Would you have shut your eyes too?

At home, the TV is off. Ma and Ama are somewhere in the dark, riding the bus back to me, following the night's spine. In my own disorganized dark, where my thoughts don't cleave to a single line, my guilt is the only thing that thrives. It writhes. My guilt is umbilical, feeding me directly, feeding me before I have a word for *need,* for *please,* for *see,* for *sever.* In the dark, in front of the shut-off screen, I lie on my belly and imagine the sofa is your body beneath mine. My fingers comb the mossed cracks between cushions, scouring for stray hairs. When I perform our past friction, my mouth fills with melon seeds. My memories all pipeline into a single reminder: *You are the predator.* Ama always told me: The best part of predation is that you get to choose your own starvation. You decide when to be merciful and when to eat. You can't blame anyone for your suffering.

I seethe, the seams of the sofa sawing through my crotch, touching my only bone. Despite my guilt, or because I want to deserve it fully, to earn a shame that would overshadow all the ones I already know, I wish I hadn't stopped when you said. What I want is to deal you a hurt so severe you will be unable to forget it, unable to wear anything else. A memory that will hunt you for your whole life, interrupting every intimacy. What I want is to hound you. To bookend my nose with the halves of your ass, inhaling to say hello. The way dogs do. To leave behind all the human ways of separating.

• • •

Once, the lovebird broke a blood feather trying to wrestle open the door of its cage. The quill was cracked and spurting blood, and because birds don't clot like us, Ma said she had to yank the feather out at the root or it would bleed forever, past death.

That night, I dreamed of the dirt field where you buried your slugs all those years ago. At first, I thought the field had regrown into grass, but the green-black blades were actually crow feathers, their quills shimmering full of salt. As I ran across the field, fleeing from the surveillance of the moon, the quills dug deeper into my feet, withdrawing my blood to feed themselves. I realized it wasn't only my feet that were bleeding: an eel of blood wove between the blades, and I followed its flicker, searching for a broken feather to yank loose. I heard Ma's echo: *To prevent a loss, a smaller one is sometimes necessary.* A small hurt to save the bird from burial. I didn't want her to pull out the feather—the bird screamed when she twisted the shaft—but she reassured me that sometimes, only pain can intercept pain.

The extracted blood feather was an ordinary loss, but the lovebird remembered it for months, and shied even from Ma's hands. I began to feel a kinship toward it, although it was prey, although it feared me more than TV explosions, more than the sound of raccoons scrabbling inside our walls. It was haunted by ordinary loss, nursing it until it grew larger than all of us, disproportionate and grotesque. The lovebird shrilled when Ma came near it at night, elasticizing the memory of injury until its fear spanned nearly a year. Its grudge outgrew the room.

It became a habit of mine to ask acquaintances if they were still friends with the girls they'd known when they were ten, five, two. More often than not, the answer was no, and when I asked why, their mouths turned slack, unable to grip anything out of the air. It was a loss so mundane it didn't even have a name. It was expected, they told me, inevitable. You were going to go to different schools eventually. Your mother was going to switch jobs. You were going to leave the city someday. You were going to move out of the neighborhood one day. You were never going to eat the hot dog I hilted in my fist, its meat unidentified, probably quilted from bits of pork bladder, the gray matter of a lesser creature. You were going to get married, feed a family. The future was grammatically a man, a flock of fingertips arriving from every direction. We were born sliding away from solitude. First comes love, then comes marriage, then comes baby in the baby carriage. It was the natural order of things, but I wanted you to challenge the chain. To shatter the link of love so that nothing else could latch onto it.

Because I wasn't brave enough to challenge it alone, I burdened you with the responsibility of being impossible. It was my fault you had to flee.

In my dreams, I cricketed in your ear canal, feasting on wax, and you walked without knowing I was inside you, your backache a growing pain. Though I prayed you were growing a second tailbone for me to ride tandem, I knew your throbbing spine was a sign you were still outgrowing me. Someday your skull would breach the lid of the sky, and another galaxy would emerge from your nasal cavity. Where was that other world? That world where we could take a break from the future? In this world, nothing could delay our separation: a daughter's job, after all, is to disperse. It was only natural to be severed from friendships. It was called growing up. Ma was wrong: being haunted was a humiliation, not a way of becoming someone's home. My longing was located only in memory. The past was my only possibility, and this was pathetic.

On the bus, I couldn't look at you, couldn't parse your presence from this scene projected onto the windows: you and me behind the birch tree at recess, knuckles of bark massaging my spine. Fear like an apple in my mouth, so sweet it split me. What if I missed your mouth entirely? What if I pissed straight to the back of your throat, where thirst was given its name? In memory, no one could say it lasted only a second, that it didn't suspend like a voice, didn't linger for weeks on the leaves. The whole incident was destined to be forgotten, swapped for clean clothes. But in memory, it was my origin story. Keeping it was my defect.

Melody was lying: imagining was not practicing, or else I would have been prepared to see you again.

In my dream of the dirt field, stubbled with blank quills, you stood ahead of me, flanked on all sides by blood feathers. *Bury me here,* you mouthed to me. *It can have my blood and not worry about losing its own. I can substitute a sacrifice.*

But I refused, kneeling instead so the quills could puncture my knees and sip me empty. The dirt field, I realized, was not made of dirt at all: it was pimple-skinned and shuddering, curved into a crow's breast. Beneath my knees, its heart bobbed up and met my wetness. Crows, you would tell me, were neither predator nor prey. We saw them scavenging, undoing the skins of everything. They were sustained by our waste. Because they confused me, I skewered their breasts with green lasers, made myself their predator. I feared my gaze would taint their feathers. But then I remembered that their plumage was incorruptible, assimilating all stains. Among a flock of crows, no one would see me. I'd hide in the night of their bodies. Pressing my palms to the fieldskin, I asked what it loved in itself, whether it was home among the living or the dead, if it knew the dog-sized crow I'd seen playing on top of the washing machine. But the crow beneath our feet must have been severed from its beak, because it didn't answer, not even in its own language, and all I could do was balance on its breath, ride the guttural rhythm of its living.

• • •

We never completed our movie. Nor did I mention it to you again, in fear that it would summon this statement: *We shouldn't be doing this.* Though it contained the word *we,* you meant it for me. It was a warning. Proof that you knew it was wrong, and I did not, and this made us different, even if we had trespassed together. Your awareness was a kind of superiority: whatever we did, you knew how to be both participant and witness. You were both inside and outside of us, creating our world and condemning it. This double act was dizzying, and I knew that if I learned it too, I might earn more time with you.

Years later, when you moved away—another one of your agong's whims, your mother complained—I heard you got a boyfriend. I wrestled this information away from the three-syllable girls whose tongues were plump as placentas, and I fed helplessly off their rumors of you, slurping straight from their veins. The only facts I could scavenge: He was a baggage handler at the airport, the one that leaned over our lives. His last name meant morning. My brother was working as a baggage handler too, and I wondered if they'd ever met. I imagined my brother sprawling your boyfriend in front of the wheels of an airplane, those wheels I imagined were tall as men. His spine would slither out of his flesh, an eel to release in a creek. I imagined my brother flinging your boyfriend into the turbine, its blades mincing him into a mound of pork. I tried to think of other ways he could be dismembered on an airfield, but I'd never seen an airplane up close, never been inside one. Ama said humans were not meant to be birds, flying this way and that way, and that if you flew too much, the air in your lungs would overflow into your arteries and cause you to float away. The anatomy of flight seemed impossible to me, and airplanes were forever the size of a pinkie. I imagined sawing his hands off at the wrist so that he'd be unable to prop up his penis when he peed. I imagined his penis in your mouth, your lips contracting into a soda-can tab, the one you taught me to whistle through by clenching it between my teeth, probing the mirrored opening with my tongue, exhaling. When I couldn't hear a whistle, you said that the song of a soda-can tab is too high to hear unless you're old or a dog, whichever comes first for us. I imagined my brother's penis in your mouth too, except my hips were stitched to it. My thumbs clung to the shoreline of your teeth. My fist docking inside your dark. In truth, I didn't know how or whether he touched you.

A year later, I got a job as a laundry attendant in the airport hotel, sorting linens by degree of soil, loading and unloading industrial machines that were stacked on top of each other. Like those silver washers, my belly was a mirror. Inside me was a fish that leaked, my innards displaced by its innards, and when I bent into the washer to peel wet towels off the walls, I thought it was your face reflected in the metallic drum. In a way, when you moved away, I was secretly relieved. It saved me from having to betray you. From having to be seen by you.

In the basement, I pressed linens with steam using a hinged machine that looked large enough to X-ray the torso of something, and a few times I burned my hands. *Steam burns are the worst kind,* Ma said, shaking her head when she saw. *Once something enters the air, it can hurt you like nothing else.*

That was the year I began to sleepwalk, and Ma and Ama found me outside most mornings, roosting on top of the washing machine, its doors flung open, our wet laundry gagged out. Once, they found me lying face up in front of the glass window, frothing green at the jaw, and they assumed I had a raccoon's rabies until they saw that my palms were heaped with detergent, my eyelashes sugared with it.

After bringing me back to consciousness, Ma sat on my futon and whispered to me: *We can't keep bringing you back here,* she said. *Someday you'll have to find your own family. Someday you'll leave me.* I flailed and said never, never, never. I writhed in her arms, feverish, upending the bowl of the night. *Why are you trying to get rid of me?* I said.

It's the natural order of things. You gave me your birth, Ma said, *and I can only give you my death. It's unfair, I know. It's a shame. We get to watch you grow, and you get to watch us die. But that's the deal. Sick, isn't it?* Her hand roamed my forehead, satelliting my sickness. In the dark, her face was wrinkled as a newborn's. *Please,* I said to myself: *Don't outgrow this moment.*

But in the morning, Ma was gone from my side, replaced by a crevice filled with sweat, and I wept. I continued sleepwalking. Ma and Ama woke up in the dark just to carry me back inside, even when I told them it was useless. In a few hours I'd find my way back under the sky, bury myself with it. They didn't know. My mouth opened. Touching that night with the back of my throat, I touched you.

• • •

Headlights lapped at the curb, the bus docking on the concrete. Without turning his head, the driver called to us, his voice arriving through a tin tunnel of soda cans, a million-ringed echo: *This is the end. You have to get out now.* Cecilia stood up beside me, her head hooking as she rubbed the knob at the back of her neck. When she took a step forward, her neck sang like a hinge, and I remembered the night she shut the door on me. She didn't look back to see if I was following. Ahead of us, the doors folded back like birds' wings, releasing a sky of fluorescent light. It faded when Cecilia and I stepped outside.

Night emptied like a bucket over our heads, drenching us in a familiar dark. The bus shelter was the only bright thing, and when the bus sped away, it looked like it was swimming off in a trench of ink, its wheels disappearing into the depths of the street. I'd never ridden this far before, and I laughed into the shimmering cold: even now, Cecilia pulled me toward the rim of myself, breaking my balance. I felt a sense of vertigo as I stood with her on the sidewalk, unmoored and floating, the bus shelter glowing like a pool of piss. I stepped deeper into its light and realized that it was sheeted on all sides by ads, one for the exterminator, her face clawed to ribbons. In fact, all sides of the bus shelter were slashed, as if some animal had lumbered up and swiped at it. Or, more likely, a flock of birds had descended, talons shredding its skin and dousing the benches with shit.

When I shifted closer, I saw daggers of shadow stabbed into the benches: they were crow feathers, glossy and hollow-quilled, brighter than the bus stop itself. A liquid, living glow, like blood still encased in its vein. This was the light lurching up my throat, thick and acidic. This was the light that said: *I cannot forgive you for forgetting. I cannot forgive us for outgrowing each other. I cannot forgive the world for its natural order.*

The raccoon-exterminating woman was holding a cage shaped like a cube, and inside it was her own severed head, her eyes vacant, her cheeks collapsed like caves. I wondered who was behind the lens when her picture was taken, who looked at her with the intent to loot.

We were alone, nowhere I knew. There wasn't a moon. As I looked up at the sky, searching for its other side, the darkness grew dense above our heads. A column of silence tucked us into its trunk. The stillness reminded me: Every silence begins inside a mouth.

Cecilia hummed, her tongue tugging on the edges of a familiar tune. She raised her head, mirroring me, and the darkness frayed into a flock of crows, descending to crown us. They sprayed onto the sidewalk ahead, perching in the dark just outside the radius of the bus shelter. She was going to follow them. In their beaks, the dark dislodged like meat, baring the blue-white marrow of tomorrow morning.

I followed her toward the crows, the flock receding from our feet. My eyes locked to the knob at the back of Cecilia's neck, and I imagined my lips around it, twisting it open. As I walked behind her, I wondered if this counted as hunting or haunting her. Maybe she would say there was no difference between the two, except for teeth and tense. It looked the same, anyway: she probed a path and I followed it tongue first. Pulled into the dark, she turned her head and smiled at me, her teeth outlasting time. Her pupils drifted across her eyes, yolks separating from their whites.

The crows gathered ahead of us. Their beaks rained down on a mound in the middle of the sidewalk. In the dark, I couldn't make out its shape, but it must have been some kind of body. Cecilia crept toward it. I joined her, worming my way under her cape of heat, but when

I looked down at the sidewalk, at the crows and their beaks hung with ornaments of meat, I couldn't tell what animal they were eating. It was skinless and twitching, a heap of green, its fat rivering into the gutter, tender as vomit. The glow of its bones, my god. Maybe it was the thing our bus had swerved to avoid earlier. Maybe it was destined to be hit and minced, no matter that we'd missed it. Cecilia and I bent over it together, the crows shifting to make room for our hunger.

I turned my head to look back at the bus stop shelter, anchoring us somewhere I'd remember. The lit-up screens reflected our faces, our gleaming beaks. When I reached up to touch my face, I felt no protrusions, no new bones inflecting my surface, and yet, when Cecilia and I looked at each other, we saw them: beaks mountaining out of our mouths, rooted to the shadows of our jawbones. Beaks shining like the perfect darkness preserved inside a belly.

Acknowledgments

Thank you to Lizzie Davis for welcoming this book whole-heartedly. This book may be small, but you made it feel significant. Thank you not only for accepting its strangeness and intensity but for encouraging me to delve even more deeply and to continue excavating its meaning. Your edits are truly incomparable, and my relationship to this book has been so joyful because of your support. Without you, *Cecilia* would be an incomplete experiment, and I'll always be grateful for your invitation to be a part of this innovative and exciting series. Thank you to my agent Julia Kardon: your expertise, savvy, openness, and willingness to guide me through every journey are always appreciated. To Abbie Phelps: thank you. Your support, communication, and thoughtful copyedits have sustained me throughout this process. My deepest gratitude to Sarah Evenson for designing a cover that is so playful and striking and nuanced. Thank you to Rachel Holscher for designing the beautiful interior. My gratitude to Chelsey Burden for her meticulous proofreading. Thank you to Mark Haber and Laura Graveline: your kind words and thoughtfulness have made this book's journey into the world so delightful. Thank you to Maya for listening to me ramble about the concept of this novella through many time-zone-crossing messages—thank you for being invested in the mess, and for the gift of your friendship.

Thank you to *Hyphen* magazine for publishing the short story that became the seed of this book. And as always, forever, thank you to my mother and to all the women in my family. Your wisdom, humor, and unsurpassable story-telling accompany me always.

Coffee House Press began as a small letterpress operation in 1972 and has grown into an internationally renowned nonprofit publisher of literary fiction, essay, poetry, and other work that doesn't fit neatly into genre categories.

Coffee House is both a publisher and an arts organization. Through our *Books in Action* program and publications, we've become interdisciplinary collaborators and incubators for new work and audience experiences. Our vision for the future is one where a publisher is a catalyst and connector.

LITERATURE
is not the same thing as
PUBLISHING

Funder Acknowledgments

Coffee House Press is an internationally renowned independent book publisher and arts nonprofit based in Minneapolis, MN; through its literary publications and *Books in Action* program, Coffee House acts as a catalyst and connector—between authors and readers, ideas and resources, creativity and community, inspiration and action.

Coffee House Press books are made possible through the generous support of grants and donations from corporations, state and federal grant programs, family foundations, and the many individuals who believe in the transformational power of literature. This activity is made possible by the voters of Minnesota through a Minnesota State Arts Board Operating Support grant, thanks to the legislative appropriation from the Arts and Cultural Heritage Fund. Coffee House also receives major operating support from the Amazon Literary Partnership, Jerome Foundation, Literary Arts Emergency Fund, McKnight Foundation, and the National Endowment for the Arts (NEA). To find out more about how NEA grants impact individuals and communities, visit www.arts.gov.

Coffee House Press receives additional support from Bookmobile; the Buckley Charitable Fund; Dorsey & Whitney LLP; the Gaea Foundation; the Schwab Charitable Fund; and the U.S. Bank Foundation.

The Publisher's Circle of Coffee House Press

Publisher's Circle members make significant contributions to Coffee House Press's annual giving campaign. Understanding that a strong financial base is necessary for the press to meet the challenges and opportunities that arise each year, this group plays a crucial part in the success of Coffee House's mission.

Recent Publisher's Circle members include many anonymous donors, Kathy Arnold, Patricia A. Beithon, Andrew Brantingham & Rita Farmer, Kelli & Dave Cloutier, Theodore Cornwell, Mary Ebert & Paul Stembler, Kamilah Foreman, Eva Galiber, Jocelyn Hale & Glenn Miller Charitable Fund of the Minneapolis Foundation, Roger Hale & Nor Hall, William Hardacker, Randy Hartten & Ron Lotz, Carl & Heidi Horsch, Amy L. Hubbard & Geoffrey J. Kehoe Fund of the St. Paul & Minnesota Foundation, Kenneth & Susan Kahn, the Kenneth Koch Literary Estate, Cinda Kornblum, the Lenfestey Family Foundation, Sarah Lutman & Rob Rudolph, Carol & Aaron Mack, Gillian McCain, Mary & Malcolm McDermid, Daniel N. Smith III & Maureen Millea Smith, Vance Opperman, Mr. Pancks' Fund in memory of Graham Kimpton, Alan Polsky, Robin Preble, Steve Smith, Paul Thissen, Grant Wood, and Margaret Wurtele.

For more information about the Publisher's Circle and other ways to support Coffee House Press books, authors, and activities, please visit www.coffeehousepress.org/pages/donate or contact us at info@coffeehousepress.org.

K-Ming Chang is a Kundiman fellow, a Lambda Literary Award winner, a National Book Foundation 5 Under 35 honoree, and an O. Henry Prize winner. She is the author of *Bestiary* (One World/Random House, 2020), *Bone House* (Bull City Press, 2021), *Gods of Want* (One World, 2022), and *Organ Meats* (One World, 2023). Her books have been *New York Times* Book Review Editors' Choice selections, included on the *New York Times* Notable Books list, and longlisted for the Center for Fiction First Novel Prize and the PEN/Faulkner Award. She can be found at kmingchang.com.

Cecilia was designed by
Bookmobile Design & Digital Publisher Services.
Text is set in Adobe Caslon Pro.